C0000 008 747 044

"I'm going to grab something to eat."

She needed to escape the urge to do exactly as he suggested—to sink into his arms and forget for the moment that she was the single mother of a very sick little boy.

"Claire." He called her name and she ignored it, turning toward the kitchen.

"I need to eat."

"No," he said. "You need a hug."

Funny how just a moment ago she couldn't cry to save her life, yet his words brought instant tears to her eyes. "Please don't."

"Don't what?"

She sucked in a breath, trying hard not to crumble because that was all it had taken—one gentle call of her name, one random act of kindness, one offer of a shoulder to lean upon—for her to lose strength.

"Don't be kind to me because if you touch me I might crumble and if I crumble I don't know if I'll be able to put all the pieces back together again."

He stared down at her with a kindness that melted her self-control. "If you crumble, I promise to help put you back together again."

His Rodeo Sweetheart

PAMELA BRITTON

First Published in Great Britain 2016
By Mills & Boon, an imprint of HarperCollins*Publishers*
1 London Bridge Street, London, SE1 9GF

Large Print edition 2016

© 2016 Pamela Britton

ISBN: 978-0-263-06606-7

Printed and bound in Great Britain
by CPI Antony Rowe, Chippenham, Wiltshire

With more than a million books in print, **Pamela Britton** likes to call herself the best-known author nobody's ever heard of. Of course, that changed thanks to a certain licensing agreement with that little racing organization known as NASCAR.

But before the glitz and glamour of NASCAR, Pamela wrote books that were frequently voted the best of the best by the *Detroit Free Press*, Barnes & Noble (two years in a row) and *RT Book Reviews*. She's won numerous awards, including a National Readers' Choice Award and a nomination for the Romance Writers of America Golden Heart® Award.

When not writing books, Pamela is a reporter for a local newspaper. She's also a columnist for the *American Quarter Horse Journal*.

This one's for Patti Mahany, the best big sister a person could ask for. You make me laugh. You've listened to me cry. You're always there for my daughter, and I appreciate that more than you know.

Chapter One

There was something about a man in uniform.

Claire Reynolds had seen a lot of them over the years. It had gotten to the point that she hardly even noticed them anymore, but *this* man, she thought as a warm wind blew off the tarmac, this man stood out— and not just because he wore dress blues.

"Ms. Reynolds?" He walked out from beneath the shade of a C-40, although he had to yell to be heard. Behind him, across a strip of asphalt that shimmered from desert heat, the nose of a C-5 cargo plane lifted. The roar of its engines sounded as if a thousand storm clouds hovered overhead.

"You must be Dr. McCall?" she all but yelled back, a hank of her long black hair blowing across her face. She should have pulled it into a ponytail.

The man nodded, his hand lifting to his hat, a black beret with a gold oak leaf cluster near the pointy tip. Major Ethan McCall. Decorated soldier. Veterinarian for the US Army. She'd been on base before thanks to CPR—Combat Pet Rescue—but she'd never met this man. Was he new?

Beneath his hat, green eyes squinted as he turned to face the back end of the smaller cargo plane, the big bay door yawning open like the back of a semi. In the shade of one of the wings, an aluminum dog crate stood silent. Claire watched as a black nose and part of a snout popped out of one of the holes, then back in again. For some reason, it made Claire smile.

She looked up at the man in uniform and found him staring at her.

"Thanks for coming all the way out here." He looked away, and Claire took a moment to gather all her hair in one hand and twist it so that it would stay in place. He was young, much younger than she had expected. And handsome. She hadn't expected that, either. Light brown hair. Strong jaw. Sideburns. A younger version of George Clooney.

"I didn't mind." And she hadn't. She'd needed to get away, even though her troubles had followed her here. As much as she loved her six-year-old son, as much as she wanted to be there for him every step of the way, she'd craved a brief burst of freedom. So she'd made the long drive east and then south to the desert, leaving Adam in the care of her brother and sister-in-law. God help her, she'd wanted to keep on driving.

"Sorry about the uniform." She looked up in

time to see something cross behind his eyes. "Funeral detail."

The reason for the heightened security presented itself. She'd been on base enough times to have the routine down by heart. But today there had been an added layer of tension. She did a half turn toward the plane and spotted it then. A casket sat just inside the cargo bay. It caused Claire's heart to stab her rib cage, the same way it did whenever she heard more bad news about her son's health.

"Oh." Of pithy things to say it probably didn't top the list, but there really wasn't much more to verbalize. He probably hadn't heard her anyway. The roar of four jet engines as they reached maximum horsepower made words disappear. When the sound faded somewhat she raised her voice and said, "I better make this quick, then."

He hadn't taken his eyes off the casket, and

when he turned back to her, she saw the sadness in them.

"It's his dog." The words emerged from her, unbidden, but when she saw him flinch, she knew it to be true.

Janus. The Belgian Malinois, which a less trained eye might ID as a German shepherd, had belonged to his friend. She had to look away for a moment, her throat closing in mute sympathy because she recognized his type of pain.

"I'm so sorry."

Her security badge caught the breeze and blew against the white shirt she wore. Inside the crate the dog poked his nose through a hole again. She was tempted to present her scent, but there would be time for that later. Instead she took a deep breath and looked Major McCall in the eye.

"Is the family certain they don't want to keep him?"

He shook his head sharply. "He's a great dog.

Passed his personality test with flying colors. It's just that the wife has two small kids. She's worried about Janus being too much to handle."

He would be a lot of work. Military dogs were known to be hyper, but they settled down once they realized their job description had changed. From military dog to family pet. It happened all the time.

She inhaled, trying to think of something else to say. "Tell them they can always change their mind."

"They won't."

He shook his head mutely. Inside the kennel Janus whined. You could tell a lot by an animal's cry. There was the feed-me whine and the I-want-out-of-my-crate whine, and the one that always tugged at her heart. The I-miss-my-master whine.

Janus wanted his master.

"Toughest part of the job, listening to their cries." She'd said the words softly, too softly to be heard by him, or so she'd thought. The cargo plane had lifted higher into the clear, blue sky, the sound of its engines slowly fading away, and the wind had caught her words, bringing them to his ears.

"It is, isn't it?" His eyes were so light that the black lashes stood out in stark contrast. From a distance it would look as if they were lined with makeup. Major Ethan McCall was all man. Wide shoulders. Narrow waist. Big hands.

She had to look away because noticing his hands seemed somehow wrong, especially given their conversation.

"I wanted to come do this for Trevor, but after tomorrow…"

She looked up again because something about his words caught her ear. She tipped her head sideways. "You're getting out?"

He nodded. "Seemed as good a time as any."

She'd met a lot of veterinarians over the years. Army. Marine. Yes, even Navy, but they were always stateside. When he glanced toward the back of the plane again, she knew he hadn't been. He'd been over there. In combat.

"Going into private practice, then?"

He shrugged. "Not sure yet."

She searched for something to say because the sadness in his eyes tore at her heart and reminded her of all she'd lost, too. Funny how you could go through life wrapped up in your own little world, feeling sorry for yourself, only to be smacked in the face by someone else's problems.

"Well, if you find yourself at loose ends, you're always welcome to visit CPR. My family owns a big ranch. You'd be welcome there."

He hadn't heard her. He kept glancing back toward a nearby hangar. The family would be here shortly, she surmised. That was the reason the base commander had stressed the importance of being on time. They wanted Janus off base so the family wouldn't have to see the dog. Less painful to them that way.

"I'll think about it," he added.

So he *had* heard her. "It's a nice drive," she said, even though a part of her warned to just shut up and get the hell out of there. "It might do you good to get out." Damn her need to mother everybody.

She was almost grateful when his gaze shifted back to Janus again. It must have served as a reminder of what they were there to do, because he braced himself. She saw the physical effects of it when he straightened his shoulders and clenched and unclenched his hands. She knew in an instant that the man whose body he'd accompanied back home had been more than a casual friend. He'd been a brother in arms. A member of his fighting family. Major McCall had been in combat, which meant someone must have pulled some strings to allow him to attend the body. She understood that type of bond all too well. She had two brothers who were military, one of them ex, the other about to be. Her husband, too, had been in the military before…

She took a deep breath. "Maybe we should get Janus loaded."

He nodded, and then turned. The dog's kennel had been placed on casters, making it easy to wheel to her vehicle. She'd been allowed to park near the tarmac, and she'd taken advantage of the shade offered by the massive metal building used to house aircraft. A local car dealership always loaned her a van for free. She chirped the lock, the two of them pausing for a moment near the double back doors.

Janus whined. She glanced at Major McCall just in time to see him swallow. Hard. "You mind if I say goodbye?"

She nodded mutely. He squatted down next to the metal box, cracked the door open.

"Shtopp," she heard him softly mutter the

German commands nearly all combat dogs grew up hearing. *"Sitz."*

Inside the kennel, Janus shifted around. She couldn't see much with the metal door blocking her view, but she spotted the black paw that landed over the top of Major McCall's hand. He turned it until the two were touching palm to pad. It made her want to cry.

"This kind lady is going to find you a new home," she heard him say. "A place where someone won't be trying to kill you every five seconds." She saw him smile bitterly. "Well, aside from maybe a five- or six-year-old kid that might try to saddle you up and ride you around."

That was so close to the truth of what might happen, Claire found herself momentarily smiling, but her smile faded fast because watching Ethan say goodbye to his friend's dog was difficult to watch. Usually a pickup was impersonal, the military staff remote. Not this time.

It took every ounce of willpower not to lose it right then and there.

"Take care of yourself, buddy." He reached in and stroked the dog's head. "Trev will be there with you every step of the way."

One last pat on the head before the man closed the kennel door. He didn't look at her as he straightened. "Can you help me lift?"

"Of course."

His hands shook as he reached for an aluminum handle. In a matter of seconds they had the crate inside. Claire stepped back and closed the doors.

"I'll take good care of him."

"I know." He still wouldn't look her in the eye. "The base commander told me about you."

"It's a labor of love."

He met her gaze and she could see it then— how hard he'd fought for control. But he had himself in hand. His eyes might be rimmed with red, but he was a soldier through and through.

A combat veteran. A man who'd been trained to keep his cool even when the world fell apart. She knew the type well.

"Thank God for people like you."

She felt close to tears again for some reason. "And thank God for servicemen like you."

They both dropped into silence, Claire wondering what he would do after today and where he would go, warning herself that it wasn't her problem.

"I should get going."

He nodded. "I'll be in touch."

She started to back away, but he held out a hand. She didn't want to clasp it. She really didn't. Stupid, ridiculous thing because there was no reason why she shouldn't, but the moment she touched him she knew she'd been right. It was like a scene from an old-time movie. A slowing down of time. A freeze-frame moment when everything seemed to stand still and all sound faded: *Zoom in camera one. Hero and*

heroine touch and seem unable to look anywhere but into each other's eyes.

"Drive carefully."

He let her hand go and smiled. He had dimples. She would have never expected dimples.

"Thanks," she heard herself say, and then
she forced herself to take a deep breath as she
turned away and headed toward the driver's side
door.

*Don't look back. Don't look back. Don't look
back.*

She looked back.

Major McCall still stood there, his hand lifting to his hat as he saluted. She smiled, saluted
back, all but wilting into the driver's seat a moment later. She started the engine and slowly
backed out, Janus whining one last time. It
wasn't until she hit the main road that she pulled
over on the shoulder.

She leaned back and closed her eyes, shaken by the touch of his hand.

"What in the world was that?"

Chapter Two

What was he doing here?

Ethan McCall looked down at his nearly finished coffee. He'd just driven five hours to pull into a strange town, order breakfast at a place called Ed's Eatery, and then sit and watch traffic pass through the small town of Via Del Caballo, California.

My family owns a big ranch. You'd be welcome there.

He recalled her eyes. They shared the same eye color, only his were nothing like her green eyes. Hers were like the rind of a lime. Bright green. Bottle green. Sun shining through glass and right into her soul green. He'd never seen anything like them before. They'd been filled with kindness, too, and maybe that's why he'd driven to her hometown. That, and the truth was, he had no place else to go.

Out in front a new car pulled into an empty parking spot, one of the diagonal kind. A small family. Two little kids. Mom laughing at something Dad said. It was such a stark contrast to his view over the past four years—crumbling buildings, half-dressed children, dust-covered cars—that for a moment he simply stared. The mom took the hand of the youngest child, a little girl with cute blond curls that caught the morning sun. Behind them and across the street, someone loaded what looked like grain into the back of their truck. The sign on the store read Via Del Caballo Farm and Feed. Out in front sat a row of livestock feeders. Round. Square. Tall. Feeders of all sizes. When he'd first sat down he'd gazed at them for the longest time, just thinking about the times he'd been in the Middle East, longing for a view like the one he had now.

Hometown, USA.

"Need more coffee?"

He glanced up at the waitress—a teenage girl with dirty blond hair and freckles—and said, "No, thanks."

She smiled and walked away, Ethan would bet she entered her pig in the county fair every year. FFA. Local rancher's daughter. Good kid with no bad habits and a weekend job.

Life in a small town. He'd fought to protect that lifestyle. Had kept going even when the chips were down. And then Trev and Janus had been shot and…

He nearly cracked the handle of his coffee mug. It took him a moment to regulate his breathing again. When he did, he glanced across the street.

And froze.

It was her. Claire Reynolds. The woman he'd come to see. The one he'd convinced himself wouldn't be home. The woman who'd called him on the phone one day—out of the blue— and asked for his opinion on a dog in her care. Behavioral issues, she'd said. But instead of calling her back he'd slipped behind the wheel of his old truck and found himself heading north and then west.

And there she was.

She'd slipped out of a pickup truck, that long, black hair he remembered so well pulled into a ponytail. She glanced toward the restaurant and he found himself turning away, even shielding his face with a hand, for some reason embarrassed even though he doubted she could see him sitting in the window of the local coffee shop. He'd felt stupid for arriving unannounced. He'd been debating with himself for over an hour whether he should call her now, drop into her place, or just go back home. Except he didn't have a home. Just an empty apartment near the base that he hated with a passion.

She'd moved to the back cab of her truck, helping a little boy down. That must be him. Her kid. The little boy who was sick. After he'd buried Trev, he'd done some calling around to find out more about the woman who now had care of Janus. He'd learned a lot about Claire Reynolds. He knew she'd started the rescue in honor of her deceased husband. They'd had trouble adopting his dog once he'd been discharged. The man had been sick and the dog had been healthy so the military had reassigned the dog—something that happened pretty frequently with wounded warriors—and so they'd lost out on the animal. The whole ordeal had prompted Claire to start Combat Pet Rescue and, when her husband had passed, to help write legislation that mandated combat veterans would have first pick at their dog. She'd thrown herself into the endeavor whole hog—

or so he'd been told. And now her son was sick, too. Cancer. Pediatrician had caught it early, but still… Some people had no luck at all.

He watched as she hugged her son, and then straightened. Her hand found the top of his ball cap, rested there for a moment, then gently stroked it, as if she'd forgotten he didn't have any hair. She snatched her hand away.

Some things just weren't fair.

Trev's wife was on her own now, too. At least she didn't have a sick kid.

He found himself standing up before he could stop to think about what he planned to do. The waitress smiled at him as he left, and Ethan nodded before sliding past the family of four and out the glass doors. It was one of those perfect Saturday afternoons. The kind made for sitting on a porch and drinking tea. Blue sky. Probably 70 degrees. The smell of summer hung in the air thanks to a sidewalk planter that held rosemary and lilac.

He headed toward the store. Up and down the street, people went about their Saturday business. It was a picturesque town. Storefront windows. Dark green canvas awnings swooping low over the sidewalks. Boutiques sat next to hair salons that sat next to antiques stores; and in front of it all, cars parked at an angle. He ducked between two of those cars now, pausing for a moment to check traffic. Just his luck to come home after three tours in the Army and get mowed down while jaywalking. The traffic on Main Street was pretty light and he made it across in time to watch Claire and her son enter the store.

"You are not getting the John Deere tractor," he heard her say. She'd disappeared between some shelves and he followed the sound. He spotted her as she made her way down an aisle filled with sprays and ointments and shampoos for animals and at the end of which lay a section of toys.

"But, Mom—"

"Don't 'but, Mom' me. You have more toys than you know what to do with."

Her son had her green eyes. He could tell because he'd stopped in front of a shelf of toys and now faced his direction. "But I don't have *this* toy."

Her ponytail swayed from side to side as she shook her head and reached for his hand. "They all look the same to me." She tugged him toward her. "Come on. I need to talk to Mr. Thomson about that shipment."

And then she faced him and froze. He did, too. Her son smacked into the back of her legs.

"Mo-om."

And it happened again. That same shock of electricity that had hit him the first time he'd seen her, out there on the tarmac, the last place he'd expected to see such a beautiful woman, one with so much sadness in her eyes.

"Hello, Claire."

SHE HAD TO be mistaken. It couldn't be—

"Dr. McCall?"

He smiled and she knew it really was. A more casually dressed Ethan in jeans and a black T-shirt and a black cowboy hat, but still the man with the green eyes that jolted her to the core. Even now she had to look away and when she did…

Scars.

Her gaze snagged on them like a hangnail. They ran up his arms. Angry red wheals criss-crossed his flesh. He had a tattoo, too, she noticed now, some type of tribal thing that circled the top of his upper left arm. They were recent, those scars, and for the first time she realized he hadn't just known the soldier who'd died, he'd been in combat with him.

"I thought I'd surprise you."

Their gazes connected again and her stomach gave that familiar lurch, the one that made her feel dizzy and uncertain and maybe even a little scared. What was it about this man? Why did being in his presence elicit such a mix of emotions?

"You surprised me, all right."

She hadn't meant her words to come out sounding so strained, but she could tell he'd picked up on the tension she felt.

"If this is a bad time—"

"No, no." Her eyes caught on Adam, who stared up at the man curiously. Her son might have recently turned six, but he had the mind of an adult, and she couldn't help but notice the curiosity in his gaze.

"Adam, this is Ethan McCall, the veterinarian I was telling you about."

"Were you in combat?"

Leave it to her son to blurt out the first thing that came to mind. He hadn't learned to filter his thoughts, but she could tell Ethan wasn't offended.

"I was." His smile was soft and easy and it

made her stomach twirl for a whole different reason. "Now I'm just a civilian."

A civilian who could help her with Thor. She shouldn't forget that. She should be grateful he'd driven all this way—and she was—she just hated the way his mere presence made her feel so out of sorts. He had that effect on her.

"My mom didn't tell me you were a real soldier."

He had wrinkles near the corners of his eyes, the kind that were so deep the skin was lighter where the cracks fanned out. Those lines disappeared as he smiled, as he did now. "Whoa there, partner. Everyone in the armed services is a real soldier."

"I know." Her son glanced up at her as if seeking reassurance. "My dad was in the Army."

"So was I."

Adam's eyes widened, and he probably would have gone on about Marcus if Claire hadn't touched his head as a way to silence him.

"So what brings you to town?" She asked the question even though she knew. Her phone call. She'd dialed his number without thinking. He hadn't called her back. Honestly, a part of her had been relieved.

When he met her gaze she spotted discomfort in his eyes, maybe even uncertainty, something she would never expect to see in a man like Ethan.

"I was thinking I could look in on that dog for you, the one that's giving you trouble. And Janus, if you still have him."

She didn't say anything. It took her a moment to realize he awaited a response. "Sure," she forced herself to say. "Absolutely." *Come on, Claire, inject a little more enthusiasm.* "That'd be great," she said with a big smile. At least she hoped it was big. And not too fake. And that it projected at least a little bit of gratitude because she really was grateful to him for making the trek all the way to her hometown.

She just wished he'd called first.

"You're going to help us with Thor?" They both glanced down at the little boy. "Man, you're brave. He almost bit my mom's hand."

Those green eyes shot to hers. "Is it that bad?"

She shifted from one foot to the other, something close to shame causing her to lick her lips in chagrin. "He's been—" she searched for the word "—a challenge."

"Then I should probably look at him sooner rather than later."

Yes, he probably should, and that was the problem because now that he stood in front of her she wondered what had possessed her to invite him to the ranch.

"You should come out today."

"Adam." Claire had to physically restrain herself from tapping her son with her toe. "I doubt Dr. McCall has time to see Thor today."

He glanced toward the door. "But I do."

"See," Adam said, taking her hand. "Let's go right now. Thor needs help."

She pulled her fingers from her son's grasp. "But I have to check on that order."

"I'll wait," he said.

She straightened. Of course he would wait. He had nothing better to do. Recently out of the Army, on his own, nobody to report to. She, on the other hand, had a million things to do, starting with her errands here in town.

She glanced down at her son, spotted the excitement in his eyes and recognized the reason for insistence. Adam felt sorry for Thor, as so many people felt sorry for her son, something she'd explained to him when he'd been given toys for no reason at all. He'd been the one to goad her into calling Dr. McCall. And here stood the good doctor, and she was grateful, she really was.

"Then I guess I'll be right back," she said, resigned to her fate. She'd just have to catch up on life another day—if she ever caught up.

Chapter Three

What was he doing?

Ethan turned down a Y in the road, following behind Claire's silver pickup, the wheels of his own truck making a sticking sound as they drove on what looked to be new pavement.

You're checking up on an old friend's dog.

They were out in the middle of nowhere, mountains ringing a picturesque valley carpeted by grass. In the distance, at the base of the hills, trees stained the bottoms a darker shade of green, but the peacefulness around him did nothing to lessen the beating of his heart. That staccato rhythm was the same type he'd felt before jumping out of a plane for the first time, or heading overseas, or facing enemy fire, and damned if he knew why he was feeling it now.

Just check in on Janus, take a look at Thor and then leave.

And go where? That was the question. That was *always* the question.

They'd traveled the road for at least a half mile, when at last Ethan spotted in the distance a small, square home that sat at the base of a low hill beneath giant oaks. A cute picket fence matched the white house. As they drew nearer, he could see a fence made of rust-colored barbed wire along the back of the property, beneath the line of trees a hundred or so yards away, the fence posts that held it in place stained gray with age. To the left of the house sat a line of kennels, at least a half dozen of them, more than one Belgian Malinois pacing inside, all of them barking up a storm. Well, all except one. He suspected that was Thor, but for now he had eyes only for Janus.

His hands gripped the steering wheel. It'd been tough saying goodbye. Tougher still to see him again. He missed Trev more than he would have thought possible given the short time they'd known each other. Then again, combat will do that to a person: make brothers out of near strangers.

"Welcome," Claire said as she stepped out of her truck.

He'd parked next to her, along the left side of her house, almost in front of the kennels. He got out and stood by the side of the truck, the smell of dirt and oak trees and fresh-cut grass so predominant that for a moment all he did was inhale.

He caught her staring at him curiously. "Nice place."

She had her hand on her son's head again, bending down to say something.

"But I want to watch him with Thor," her son said.

"In a minute," he heard her murmur.

The boy's head bowed. His shoulders slumped. He did everything but kick at a rock, but he did as she asked, muttering something under his breath, something about Hawkman.

His gaze must have reflected his puzzlement because she smiled. "His immune system still isn't up to par." Her smile faded a bit. "He thinks I'm stupid for wanting him to go inside and wash his hands after we've been out and about."

"So he's threatening to have Hawkman come after you?"

The smile turned back on. "He's a friend of the family."

"You have a superhero for a friend?" For the first time since his arrival, he felt like smiling, too. "Wow. I'm impressed."

Something low and soft that he recognized as a laugh filled the air. "Not really. We're friends with Rand Jefferson." She shook her head. "The actor that plays the superhero in the movies. It's a long story."

"Maybe you can tell it to me after I say hello to an old friend."

"Yeah, sure." Her smile seemed to have a short in it because it fizzled. "He's over there."

"I know."

Janus had spotted him. He could tell by the way the dog's eyes had fixated on him, his whole body having gone still, as if he silently tried to telepathically commune with his old friend. He knew what he would say.

Where have you been? What are you doing here? Where's Trevor?

He didn't have an answer for the dog.

"Platz," he ordered sternly as dog after dog jumped up on the fence of their loafing sheds. Janus just stood there, as if he tried to reassure himself through sight and smell that it really was his master's old friend. Then he shifted his gaze past Ethan, as if hoping to spot Trev.

He nearly stumbled.

I keep looking for him, too.

You deployed with someone. You see them day in and day out. You drink beers with them, you shoot pool with them, you even go on leave together once or twice. And then—*bam*—just not there. He still couldn't believe it. He couldn't imagine how Janus felt.

"How are you?" he asked the dog, flipping up the latch that kept the front gate closed. "Good to see you again, buddy."

The familiar words set the dog's tail in motion. He still glanced behind Ethan again, then he sat down in front of him.

Ethan smiled. This, too, was familiar. When Trevor would bring Janus in for a post-op exam, the dog would walk right up to him and sit down, as if silently saying, "Go on. Get it over with."

"Nah," he said softly, squatting down in front of him. "I don't need to check you for bullet wounds. Not here. Not today."

Not ever again.

His hands had started to shake again. He covered the tremors by burying them in Janus's fur. It wouldn't hurt to check the condition of his injuries, he told himself, parting the fur, finding a diagonal slice that started at the top of his right shoulder blade and ended between his two front legs. A piece of mortar had nearly taken his leg off, but it was healing nicely.

"How does he look?"

Ethan didn't turn, just went on exploring Janus's body as he said, "Good."

He dragged his hand along the dog's side where he found a half-dollar-sized bump. Sniper round. Went clean through. Miracle Janus had lived. Another scar on his other side—this was from an old bomb blast. So many untold stories. So many near misses. Until…

He stood quickly. Janus scooted closer to him, his head tipped back, dark eyes unblinking. He opened his mouth and started to pant, something close to a canine smile lifting the corners of his mouth as their gazes locked.

I missed you, too, he silently telegraphed.

But it was also damn difficult. It brought it all back. The trip home. The funeral afterward. The look on Trevor's wife's face as she'd been handed the flag. She tried to be so strong for her kids, but her hands had trembled as she reached for the talisman, and he'd watched as the weight of her sorrow brought down the roof of her control.

"Ethan?"

"Whatever you're doing, keep on doing it."

Breathe, he told himself. *And again. Don't let Claire see how close you are to crumbling, too.*

"Good. I'm glad. Just as soon as he's healed from his wounds, I've got a home lined up for him."

He had to work to keep his voice even. "He'll do great." He just wished…

"What?"

Clearly she'd read the dissatisfaction in his eyes. "I wish she would have taken him."

"Who?"

"Naomi," he clarified. "Trevor's wife. I wish she would have taken him."

"Me, too."

He should have applied to take Janus home, but that was the problem. He didn't have a "home," a necessary component to being approved for adoption. He might have been able to pull some strings, but to be honest, then what? He had no idea where he was going, or what city he'd end up in, or what he'd end up doing. Before he'd left for Via Del Caballo he'd applied to a number of jobs, most of them working at veterinary clinics, but a few of them doing what he wanted to do—training dogs. Right now, Janus didn't fit into his life. Better to let him go, to let him start over with a family to love him.

"Ready to look at Thor?"

"Sure."

The dog hadn't changed position since his arrival. He still lay huddled against the wall of his shelter. He couldn't even see the dog's eyes, they were buried so deeply into his paws.

"I put him on the end so I could interact with him on my way to and from the kennels." She led him back the way they'd come. "It hasn't helped. He's snapped at me twice. I usually don't neuter them right away, but I'm wondering if it wouldn't help with this dog. To be honest, I'm at my wit's end."

He approached the dog warily, his experience with military working dogs—or MWDs—having taught him that it was often better to approach behind the safety of a fence first, so he once again walked around the corner of the row of kennels. All the dogs had passed a behavioral test, but still, she had a point. Neutering him might help, too. In fact, most MWDs were adopted out already spayed or neutered, but Claire took all dogs in, one of the rare civilian operations in the United States. Clearly, someone had pulled some major strings when setting up her operation, not that he cared. As long as the dogs were well taken care of. Thor looked good, he thought, approaching the kennel. Beneath the shade of a giant oak tree, the dog blended in with a shadow but his coat and his weight told Ethan all he needed to know. His lack of movement told him something, too; he was a dog that clearly didn't want to be disturbed.

"He's obviously eating well."

"He is, but he waits to eat until I'm not around. I've watched him through my kitchen window. He picks at his food, too, I've noticed, eating a little here and a little there."

"Any vomiting or diarrhea?"

"No. I had him checked out by a friend. She did a complete workup. Nothing wrong."

He squatted down next to the dog's run. "Hey, Thor, buddy. How's it going?"

No response. Not an ear twitch. Not a wrinkled nose. Not even a tiny wag of the tail.

"What happened to his partner?"

"KIA."

It was just a phrase—KIA—but it kicked him in the gut. He had to grab at the fence as the familiar anxiety returned, not that Thor noticed. Ethan could still smell the desert if he closed his eyes. Hear the sound of the incoming mortar just before it hit their encampment. Hear the screams…

Stop.

He couldn't change the past. Couldn't change what happened to Trevor any more than he could change the direction of the wind. He took a deep breath, inhaling the scent of oak and pollen-filled air and…Claire.

Mostly, he focused on the smell of Claire; vanilla with maybe just a hint of butterscotch thrown in. Woman were a rarity over there, especially pretty women, women who smelled good. He would focus on her and her kind eyes.

Three, two...

He got ahold of himself, just as he'd taught himself to do, with grim determination. His hands still shook, but he was able to focus on the dog again. "Do you have a whistle?"

"Do I..." He turned in time to spy her look of consternation. "In the house, I think."

"Would you get it for me?"

She turned without another word, and Ethan watched her walk away. The scent of her lingered. Like dessert after Sunday dinner. Like home.

You are home, idiot. Back in the States.

No. Like when he'd grown up with his grandfather, back before he'd died. The best times of his life. And then everything had changed.

And if she knew how messed up you are, she'd stay in her house. To hell with the whistle.

That was the thing; nobody knew how messed

up he was. Not even his superior officer. Not even the military shrink. Not even the discharge officer who'd asked him repeatedly if everything was okay.

No. Things weren't okay. And it scared the heck out of him.

SHE FOUND A whistle with Adam's help, her son insistent that he go outside and watch whatever it was Major McCall was about to do.

"Do you think he'll have him attack someone or something? You know, blow the whistle and tear something to shreds."

Her son might be bald. He might still be recovering from the hell the doctors had put him through to kill the cancer in his blood, but he was still a boy.

"No, Adam. I don't think he's going to do that."

They emerged into the bright, spring sunshine. It'd been a year ago that Adam had been diagnosed. A year ago since her world had fallen apart. Hard to believe time had passed so quickly, but they weren't out of the woods yet. Though the cancer hadn't metastasized, it was still a waiting game. So far the immune depression therapy had worked, but they still had a while to go before they'd be given the all clear—*if* they were given the all clear. Things could change at any moment, which was why she refused to get her hopes up.

"What's wrong with him?" Adam asked Ethan, his baseball cap nearly falling from his head he bounced up on his toes so hard. "Are you going to put him through his paces?"

She had to give him credit; Ethan didn't seem bothered by her son's exuberance. Quite the contrary. He smiled down at him, even tapped the brim of his hat, just as she did, and it was then she noticed it.

His hands shook.

Her eyes shot to his. Was he nervous? Did Thor make him afraid?

"I'm just going to perform a little test." He held out his hand for the whistle.

Yes. No mistaking it. He shook.

"Here." The polished surface caught the light as it swung back and forth.

He snatched the whistle from her so fast she wondered if he knew she'd spotted his quaking limbs. Something about the way he turned away from her, too, as if he were afraid she'd look too closely. Little did he know. The man had held her attention since the moment she'd met him.

He blew the whistle.

Loudly. Shrilly. Unexpectedly. Claire's heart nearly jumped from her chest.

"Ouch." Adam covered his ears. "That was loud."

And Thor didn't move.

Claire stood, frozen, as a dozen little puzzle pieces fell into place. The way the dog ignored her. How he never rushed to greet her when she went outside. How he never came to her when she called his name.

He was deaf. She felt like a fool for never checking something so basic, so in-your-face obvious. Then again, Thor had been given a full physical, and a health clearance following that. He still bore the physical scars of his injuries. She'd just assumed his lack of attention was related to the physiological baggage he carried.

She took a step closer to Ethan and said, "It wasn't just his unresponsiveness that concerned me. There are other…issues, too."

He tucked the whistle in his pocket. "Like what?"

"He seems…detached somehow. He never wags his tail. Barely shows interest in his food. Ignores me for the most part."

He headed toward the entrance to the kennel.

She rushed to catch up to him. "Let me go in with you."

Adam knew to stay behind. He'd been strictly forbidden from dealing with Thor, but that didn't stop him from asking, "Can I go in, too?"

"No," she told her son. "Stay here."

She patted him on the head again, something she seemed to do more and more of late. Reassuring herself that he was still there. At least that was what one of the other moms at the hospital had told her when she'd spotted the gesture.

Ethan had rounded the end of the building. He didn't seem the least bit concerned about Thor's behavior.

Still, she heard herself say, "Be careful," as he slipped inside the "doghouse," as Claire liked to call it, a spacious room with a man-sized door leading to the dog run. Inside, an uneaten bowl of food lay in the corner. It worried her. Every day she hoped the dog would get better. Now she didn't know what to think.

Thank God he made a house call.

Fate, she admitted.

Thor lay just outside the back door, and Ethan moved slowly, his footfalls light. There had been dozens of times when Claire had done the same and she'd always taken care to use a soft voice to announce her arrival. Now she understood why the dog had been startled to the point that he'd tried to bite her. She'd snap at someone, too, if she'd been taken by surprise.

"Hey, Thor," she heard Ethan say. When she joined him, it was in time to see Ethan kneeling by the dog's side, but this time the dog's reaction was different. Normally he cocked an eye, maybe lifted his head in mute greeting, then went back to ignoring the world. This time he opened his eyes, immediately lifted his head, then stood. He moved toward the man who knelt beside him and sniffed, only to be clearly disappointed by his investigation. The dog's head lowered. His shoulders appeared to slump. He lay down at Ethan's feet.

"He's missing his handler," Ethan observed.

His *male* handler, she realized. She was just a poor second in the dog's eyes. Not worth getting to know.

"He was injured pretty severely," she said. "I'm thinking he probably lost consciousness. I would imagine he has no clue what happened to him."

"Yeah, I had a friend send me his file."

He'd done that for her? For the dog? Somehow, that took her by surprise.

He buried his fingers in the dog's fur, held them there for a moment, and if she hadn't been watching him closely, she might have missed the way he inhaled deeply. It was as if the dog's presence reassured him. He ran his fingers through Thor's coat, and she wasn't sure if it was a professional gesture, or a personal one. Another deep breath and then he began to move his hands up and down the dog's body, feeling for the scars now covered by hair, she realized. Another dog that'd been injured by a bomb blast. She'd seen far too many in the past three years. Thor had nearly had his leg taken off. The missing patch of fur right below the knee was the only visible sign of his injuries.

She knelt down next to Thor, too, touching him. Whatever Ethan's problem was, she understood all too well the soothing reassurance of a dog's coat. How many times had she come out and done the same thing, sometimes in the middle of the night, her son completely oblivious to her midnight visits?

"Anything?" she asked.

He shook his head.

Their gazes met and there it was again. The sadness. It lingered in his eyes like a bad stain. "No sign of pain anywhere. That's good." He went back to examining the dog.

She had to inhale deeply, too, but for another reason. What was it with this man, that she found herself studying him just as intently as he examined Thor?

He seemed to have recovered himself now. He cupped the dog's head. Thor looked up at him obediently. "We always do a complete physical before releasing a dog to civilian life, but it's entirely possible the loss came later." He lifted the dog's lips, checking gum color. "Scar tissue can do more damage than the initial injury."

Satisfied with what he saw in the dog's mouth, he examined Thor's ears next.

"So what now?"

"Damn. I wish I were back on base with all my instruments."

"Do you need me to make a call? My brother's wife has a friend who's a vet, and she could bring her truck over."

"No. That's okay." He moved Thor's head so he could peer into the left side ear. "I can't see any obvious obstruction. I'm betting scar tissue."

He held the dog's head again, lifting an index finger and seeing if Thor tracked his progress, similar to what a human doctor would do. His hands had stopped shaking. He had gone into full-on doctor mode.

"Looks good. I was thinking some kind of lingering pain might be causing his lack of appetite, but that's not it. He's unresponsive to pressure test, and his teeth look good, so no abscess in the mouth."

He moved in closer to the dog, sat down next to him, stroking his head. Thor did something she'd never seen before then; he placed his head in the man's lap. She saw Ethan freeze, and then his expression changed. His face softened as he silently communicated reassurance with his hand. And just like his human counterpart, the dog inhaled deeply and closed his eyes.

Claire wanted to cry.

"What's the matter, buddy?" Ethan said to the dog.

She moved in closer. "Sometimes I wish they could talk."

He stroked Thor's head absently. "Well, if they could, this one would probably tell us he's depressed."

"Is that possible?"

"They're a lot like humans."

"So what do we do?"

"It'll take some time for him to adjust, and to come out of his depression."

"*If* he comes out of it," she added.

He nodded and Claire's heart dropped. If he wasn't in perfect health she couldn't adopt him out to a new family. Well, she could, but it'd be more difficult to place an animal with issues. Nearly impossible, as a matter of fact. There would be interviews and screening and maybe even a trial period. Time. That was what it would take.

"Is he going to need special help?"

She'd forgotten about her son with his nose

pressed up against the chain-link fence, but his words tore at her heart. "Special help" was what she called his cancer treatment. She hated the C word, avoided using it at all cost.

"He'll need special training," Ethan said, "to compensate for his lack of hearing. He's used to listening for commands so we have to teach him to look only for nonverbal commands, arm movements. The good news is he already knows most of them. We'll have to teach him some new ones, and teach him to constantly keep his gaze focused on his handler, but retraining him is possible. No more walking up to him unannounced. Make sure he sees you before you touch him. That should stop the biting."

"That's easy," Adam said. "I can do the training, too."

Claire shook her head at her son. "Honey, it's not as easy as that. It'll take a professional. What Dr. McCall is suggesting isn't like teaching a dog to sit and stay. He'll need to learn to listen without hearing. That means he can never be out of his kennel. If he can't hear he won't be able to hear us and learn boundaries. What if he ran into the woods?"

There was nothing but open land between the ranch and the coast. Well, that wasn't precisely true. There were coastal towns, but the point being, if Thor got out, they'd be lucky if they ever found him again.

"I'll help him learn." Adam's soft words pricked at her heart. Alas, her son was in no condition to take on the task of training a dog.

"No." She made sure her word was firm. "We'll have to find someone else to retrain him."

"I know someone." Ethan straightened.

Claire's heart jumped in relief. "Who?"

The wrinkles next to his eyes reappeared. "Me."

Chapter Four

She couldn't have appeared more shocked if he'd announced his intention to drive his car to the moon.

"You?"

He faced her squarely. "I was thinking earlier that I might be able to help you out. At least for a little while, until I decide where I'm going next."

Green eyes that were so beautiful he couldn't stop studying them blinked, then blinked again. She had the world's longest lashes, the tips of them touching the arch above her eyes. Sweeping black brows dropped down low in consternation.

"But you have your own life to get back to."

"What life?" As sad as it sounded, it was true. Why else had he driven a hundred miles to see her? "I'm in between jobs right now, trying to decide which direction I want to go. I've actually been toying with the idea of training dogs, my way of still helping our country. I'd still practice medicine, but I'd like to learn that aspect of military dogs. Finding that type of job might take a little while, though. In the meantime I have a bit of money and plenty of time on my hands. Let me help."

She started to shake her head, that pretty, silky black hair of hers falling over one shoulder, but her son interrupted her midshake.

"He could stay with Uncle Colt."

She whirled around to face the boy. "Adam, no. We couldn't impose on your uncle like that.

Besides, your other uncle, Chance, will be coming home soon. He'll need the apartment then."

"But he won't be home for three more months. You said so yourself." The boy's lower lip jutted out, green eyes imploring. "They have that super big place and it's empty."

"Yes, but they won't want a stranger staying there."

"Major McCall isn't a stranger."

"Adam—"

"It's okay." Ethan smiled down at her son. "I can find a place in town."

But the little boy's eyes showed grim determination. "I'll go call Uncle Colt right now."

The boy turned toward the house, calling over his shoulder, "He won't mind."

"Adam!"

She'd been ignored. He saw her mouth open and close a few times. Claire clearly wanted to call to her son again, maybe even run after him.

Instead she stood there, something close to em-barrassment floating through her eyes.

"I'm sorry."

"What for?" It was hard not to smile in the face of determination like Adam's, but he had a feeling if he showed her his amusement, Claire would feel even worse. "I think he's trying to help."

"You're probably right. Ever since he's been sick he's been worried about me. He says I do too much. That I'm always busy and it's not good for me. He's such a little man but he has grown-up concerns."

Her words had the ability to make him forget his own troubles for a moment. He'd almost bro-ken down earlier. But he'd stopped it—thank-fully. And here was her son, fighting for his life. It served as an example that there were worse things in life than dealing with a little anxiety.

A little?

Okay. Some days he would swear he was

about to have a heart attack, and as he stared into Claire's kind eyes, he wondered what she would do if she knew the truth—that the man who was at her place to "help" needed help of his own.

A screen door slammed.

"That was quick," she said.

Adam didn't run, but his steps could almost be called a skip. Ethan knew what his uncle's answer had been before Adam even spoke.

"He said to bring him over." His smile could have lit up the inside of a room.

"Adam—"

"He said he thinks it'd be cool to have a dog doctor living on the property."

Claire's mouth opened and closed again. He could tell she wanted to say something, to dash the boy's hopes with words, but she wasn't proof against the excitement in her son's eyes.

"I take it he lives at Misfit Farms?" Ethan asked, having passed a sign along her driveway that pointed to a different road, one labeled with that name.

She nodded.

"I don't mind going over there." He tried to tell her without words that he wasn't about to take advantage of her brother's kindness. He knew she didn't want him to and he would respect that wish. "You can show me around the place."

She must have received the message because some of the concern faded from her eyes. She still searched for something to say, though, something that she could use to finagle her way around her son's high-handedness.

Something wet touched his hand.

He looked down. Thor peered up at him, curiosity in his brown eyes. Ethan glanced at Claire. Her eyes had gone wide.

"He likes you."

No. He probably reminded Thor of his handler, the man who'd been killed in action...*like Trevor.*

"See." Adam's eyes were as wide as his mom's. He pointed. "Thor wants you to stay, too."

Claire stared up at him, then down at the dog, then back at him again.

She looked troubled, and resigned. "Maybe you should go meet my brother."

Thor's nose nudged his palm again.

Maybe he should.

THEY DROVE TO her brother's place in less than two minutes. Claire tried to ignore the presence of the man in the seat next to her, but it was nearly impossible.

Thor liked him.

For the first time since the dog had arrived she'd seen life in the canine's eyes. What did it mean? Would Ethan be able to get through to the dog, something nobody else had been able to do? She could tell Ethan didn't plan to accept the invitation to stay with her brother, and she appreciated his tactfulness, yet suddenly she wondered…

His hands had shaken.

There had been that look in his eyes, too, the one she'd recognized. She seen the same look in her husband's eyes when he'd come home from the war, and then later, as he'd been admitted to the hospital. The same look in her son's eyes.

Fear.

He fought demons, this man who had suffered through war. It made her want to help him. Marcus had called it her greatest gift— her desire to help. Claire thought of it more as a weakness because she often stretched herself too thin thanks to her inability to say no. It was why she'd gotten into the dog rescue business. Why she'd insisted on nursing her husband herself even though the military had offered hospice care. Why she'd stayed by her father's side, too, even though she had owed the man nothing.

Her tires hummed as she drove over the newly paved road. She couldn't get used to the smoothness, but Natalie, her brother's new wife, had insisted her clients would expect pavement. Still, as she turned left toward Colt's place, she wondered what the cows that still ranged the pastures thought about the strange black strip.

"Wait until you see my uncle's place." Adam leaned forward, as if they would have a hard time hearing him when his voice was just one level above a yell over the sound of the truck's diesel engine. "It's awesome."

Awesome was one word. *Expensive* another. *Amazing* was applicable, too. Her sister-in-law had won a huge jumping event last year, one with an equally huge purse. Natalie must have spent nearly all of it building her new riding facility.

"Wow," Ethan said when they drove between

two low-lying hills, and her brother's place came into view.

Wow was right. The big red barn still stood in the same spot as it had in their youth, as did the house directly ahead, but the two-story farmhouse had been given a new coat of white paint. The original barn—the one she and her brothers had hidden from their father in when they were younger—had been converted back to a hayloft. Directly opposite it now, to their left, sat a gorgeous twenty-stall barn that seemed to match the old-fashioned farmhouse somehow. It was two stories, four windows with wooden frames directly above the opening—the apartment her brother Chance would live in one day soon.

That wasn't the only big change.

A covered arena sat behind the barn. A white fence surrounded the whole complex. They had to pass between the pristine posts, her truck's wheels catching the newly installed cattle guard and vibrating the interior.

"That always makes my insides jiggle," Adam said with a giggle.

Hers, too, she admitted, marveling at how green it all was now. Sprinklers. They sprayed every surface that wasn't covered by asphalt, including the square turnout pastures by her brother's old arena to her right. The "outdoor arena" they called it now. There were a few jumps in the middle of it, but the bulk of her sister-in-law's practice fences were in the covered arena. That was because her brother still managed Rodeo Misfits, his specialty act that involved trick riding. They needed the arena for practice. Still, the whole place was like an emerald gem set in the middle of a golden field.

"Does your family compete in riding competitions?"

"You could say that."

"My uncle is a rodeo performer. My aunt jumps horses."

All of which should be self-evident to some degree, Claire thought. Though it was the middle of the week, no less than four people rode in the covered arena, one of them her brother, looking out of place in his Western saddle among all the English riders. His truck and trailer still sat in the same spot, though, the words *RODEO MISFITS* still emblazoned on the sides. At least that hadn't changed.

"This is some place."

"That's the apartment." Adam pointed to the windows above the opening of the barn.

"Adam, we don't even know if Dr. McCall wants to stay with us yet."

Adam all but poked his head between the two front seats. "You do, don't you, Major McCall?"

"It's Dr. McCall," he corrected. "I'm out of the Army now. And I'd love to stay here, but I think we need to talk to your uncle first."

Points in the man's favor for being diplomatic. She had to focus on keeping her gaze straight ahead, though. The urge to look at him, to smile, to reach out to this man in a way that was personal, was nearly overwhelming.

"Uncle Colt said he'd get off his horse when we got here."

He must have called her brother on his cell. Determination, thy name is Adam.

They parked in front of the new barn and it still felt strange to slip out of her truck and hit pavement. Natalie had explained that her wealthy clients didn't like dirt and mud, something that seemed stupid considering they rode horses, but she didn't doubt her sister-in-law for a minute. People who jumped horses tended to be wealthy and drive cars that cost six figures. Prissy people, her brother called them, though he'd become friends with most of them in the past year.

Adam was already on his way through the

middle of the barn and the arena on the other side. Prissy people didn't like to get wet, either, which was why they'd erected the covered arena less than twenty yards from the back entrance of the barn.

"This place is amazing," Ethan repeated.

Claire nodded. "I've been afraid to ask how much it all cost."

It even smelled new. New paint. New shavings. New leather. Shiny leather halters straddled brass hooks. She couldn't see any of the horses inside, not at first—the metal grates along the front stopped them from poking their heads out—but as she walked down the center aisle, one sleek animal after another was revealed. Some ate. Some stood. Some peered at her curiously as she walked by.

"Beautiful animals."

"Imports," Claire explained. "Most of them, at least. Although there's a few off-the-track

Thoroughbreds and even a quarter horse or two. The majority were bred in Europe."

"I used to see horses when I was in veterinary school, although nothing like this."

He walked next to her along the barn aisle, light shining on his face despite the cowboy hat, thanks to the opening at the other end of the barn. He'd tucked his hands in his jeans. She wondered if his hands shook again and had to fight the urge to turn her head and study him intently. Whether he suffered from anxiety or not, it was none of her business. She appreciated his help, but no more than that.

"You worked on horses in the military?" She glanced at him.

"Cavalry units. Believe it or not, they're still in existence, although they're mostly for parade purposes."

"These horses are strictly for jumping and some of them cost as much as a new house."

"I don't doubt it."

Her sister-in-law received a commission on sales. Between that and her purse earnings she'd been able to build everything around them. It drove Colt nuts. Her brother was very much a man, and the fact that his wife made more money than he did took some adjusting, but they made it work. Her brother had found love and she couldn't be happier for him.

"Mom, Uncle Colt says Major McCall can stay in the apartment above the barn if he wants."

Her brother sat on a horse on the other side of a solid-wood rail, a wide smile on his face, Adam having already accosted him. Not for the first time she noticed how much he'd changed. His gold eyes always seemed lit from within. His black hair was tucked beneath a black cowboy hat—as it always was—but he didn't keep it as closely shaved as he used to. More relaxed, that's what he seemed. And happy. Very, very happy. She doubted their brother, Chance, would recognize him when he came home in a few months.

"I take it you're Major McCall," Colt called out to her guest.

"Ethan," the handsome doctor said—yes, handsome, damn it. It wasn't a crime to notice. "Nice to meet you."

The two shook hands, although her brother had to lean over the rail to do so, not that the horse he rode seemed to mind. Playboy—her sister-in-law's horse—she recognized, the horse's successful reining career having resulted in Colt hitting fewer rodeos and staying closer to home. He still loved his rodeo act, but he loved his new wife more. That was why he'd turned the act over to someone new—Carolina Cruthers—although Claire wasn't quite sure what to make of the standoffish woman.

"My nephew told me you just got out of the military."

"Been out two weeks," Ethan clarified.

"So this is him?" Her sister-in-law rode up next to her husband, a wide smile on her face, blond hair tucked beneath a black-and-gray helmet.

"This is him," Claire echoed, for some reason incredibly self-conscious. Maybe it was because she knew Natalie had noted the doctor's good looks. There was a twinkle in her blue eyes as their gazes connected, and a nonverbal, "No wonder you want him to stick around."

It's not like that, she silently telegraphed.

Okay, so maybe it was. She was human and it'd been a long, long time since she'd been with a man. So long, in fact, that she couldn't even remember that far back. Scratch that. She remembered. About a year after her husband had died. A quick hookup the weekend of the town rodeo, and a night she'd rather forget, but it served to remind her of yet one more reason why she'd never let her attraction to the man get out of hand. Awkward couplings in the middle of the night weren't her thing.

Not even when the man was as handsome as Ethan.

At least, that was what she told herself.

Chapter Five

"I'm Natalie Reynolds," said a woman on a massive sorrel horse. She held out a hand wearing an odd-looking glove. Half leather, half crochet. "And this is my husband, Colt, since Claire seems too distracted to perform the introductions."

Ethan glanced at Claire in time to see her eyes flick away, seemingly in humiliation, but what did she have to be embarrassed about?

"Nice to meet you." Ethan shook Natalie's hand, her horse snorting in protest at the sudden thrust of his arm. Might be big, but the horse still had the nerves of a Thoroughbred.

Couldn't deny it was a beauty, though. The animal looked almost wet its coat glistened so noticeably. When Claire had said her sister-in-law's horses were worth a small fortune, she hadn't been kidding.

"You're the dog doctor, Adam tells me," the woman said.

"MWDs—military working dogs."

She nodded, her eyes the same color as a military ribbon. They projected friendliness, those eyes. "Ever work on horses?"

"Actually, yes." Most people were like Claire. They had no clue that military veterinarians worked on all sorts of different animals. It all depended on the base where they were stationed. He could look at a cat one day, a bird the next, sometimes even cows. All that had changed, however. "I was attached to a cavalry unit once, nonactive, strictly for parade purposes, but it was fun traveling around with them."

That was before. Pre-orders. Off to the Middle East. Life had never been the same since.

"Interesting," Natalie said.

"But I'm not really tied to my veterinary career. My hope is to work for one of the big canine training facilities. I'd like to keep serving my country in a small way and that seems like the best way to do it."

Claire looked impressed, then thoughtful. "That explains why you're so willing to work with Thor."

He forced himself to focus on Claire's words, because that was who'd spoken. He stared into her eyes, observed the different specks of green in them. A distraction technique, one that he hoped would keep his hands from shaking yet again.

"That's part of my master plan, anyway," he admitted.

Focus.

He'd been hoping—damn, how he'd been hoping—a trip to the country might be just what his frazzled nerves needed. He realized too late he'd been kidding himself. Trev's death was still too fresh. The things he'd witnessed still in the forefront of his mind. The helplessness he'd felt was something he would never forget.

Damn it.

"I think it might actually work out to have him stay here," he heard Natalie say.

"No," he interjected. Natalie drew back a bit and he realized he'd sounded a little terse. "Look, you're really kind to even consider offering me a place to stay." He caught the boy's gaze, forcing a smile. "But I can't accept."

"Actually, you'd be doing us a favor."

It was Claire's brother who'd spoken, the man leaning forward and resting an arm on his saddle's horn, saddle creaking in protest. "One of the owners Natalie rides for has decided to put her horse up for stud. We were just talking about how to handle that." He pointed with his chin at his wife. "We both know a lot about horses, but we're not breeding experts, and the stallion in question is worth a lot of money. We have a friend who's a vet, but she's pregnant and busy, and we have no business risking its health in the breeding shed, and so we need a professional to help us do it right. At least until we can find someone to do it permanently."

Natalie was nodding as she fiddled with her reins. "I was explaining to my husband just yesterday that a lot of big show barns offer stallion service." A strand of blond hair had escaped from beneath the black cap she wore. "It was kind of a long-range plan of ours to do the same, and then my owner called last week and she really doesn't want to have to move her horse…"

"So we were thinking this would work out perfectly," Colt finished. "We'd hire you as a consultant. You could advise us on what equipment to buy and what kind of facility we'll need. And if you're still here after we get it all done, you could be our stallion manager, at least until you decide to move on or we find another full-time veterinarian interested in the job. In between all that, you could work as our barn manager. You know, keep an eye on things when we're gone on the weekends."

"See?" Adam's voice was full of smug satisfaction. "All settled."

Ethan had a feeling the words were something Claire said on a regular basis and that Adam just parroted. Still, their offer was too generous to believe. "You really want me to work here?" He turned and anchored his gaze on Claire's again. She seemed just as surprised as he did.

"Well, maybe." Natalie splayed a hand in his direction. "We realize we only just met you, and this is way sudden. It's sudden for us, too, so worst-case scenario, why don't you stay a night and think about it? Adam tells us you're kind of homeless right now."

He was, but he still couldn't take them up on such a generous offer.

"Look, it's really nice of you to offer, but I wouldn't be comfortable imposing."

"You wouldn't be imposing," Colt said. "You're a brother in arms. Or didn't you know I was in the Army, too? I wouldn't dare let a combat veteran stay in a strange hotel, not when we have a perfectly good place for you to bed down for the night."

"There's an apartment over the barn." Natalie's smile grew. "It's nothing big, but it's new and it's perfect for a single man. Colt and Claire's brother will be living there when he gets discharged in a few months."

"Please?" Adam said, coming up and smiling at him. "It'd be a big help to my mom."

He realized then that the boy didn't want him to stay for selfish reasons. This wasn't about having a cool new adventure learning how to train dogs. This was, and always had been, about making sure his mom didn't have to deal with Thor all on her own. The boy worried about his mother, just as she probably worried about him. They were looking out for each other. He had no idea why that made him feel weird inside, but it did.

He inhaled deeply. He didn't want to do it. There were a million reasons why he shouldn't— his recent anxiety attacks, his horrible dreams, his need to get on with his life, but most of all, his hatred of being a burden on people.

But there was one reason why he *should* do it. Actually two.

He looked into Claire's eyes, and then her son's.

"Okay. I guess I'll stay."

"YOU SHOULDN'T HAVE made such a big deal about it." Claire stared at her son. Thank God they were back in her own house and Ethan at her brother's place. "The poor man probably felt so guilty about saying no, he didn't think he had a choice."

Her son sat in the same chair he had when she'd broken the news to him about his illness a year ago. He'd lost his hair somewhere in between, but the light from the kitchen window behind him revealed a peach-fuzz scalp. He looked better. Less pale. Maybe a little more flushed than she would like to see, but so much better than at the start of this whole mess.

"Well?" she asked, because he just sat there staring up at her.

"You need help, Mommy."

The kid knew how to work her, that's for sure. All he had to do was call her mommy.

"No, I don't need help. We have plenty of help between Uncle Colt and Aunt Natalie and their friends. And Uncle Chance will be back soon. We're fine."

"Uncle Colt and Aunt Natalie are too busy, and Uncle Chance isn't coming home for three more months." He said three more months as if it were a whole lifetime, and in his world, it probably was. "One more person would be good. You could go to town and things."

Go to town: code words for *stop worrying about me.* He might be six, but her son had the wisdom of someone five times his age. She couldn't help worrying about him, though. The doctors watched Adam like a hawk. Blood samples could be taken locally, but they made the trip to Los Angeles to speak to his oncologist about the results and any adjustments that would need to be made to the myriad of medications they had him on. It served as a constant reminder that her son was in a battle for his life. So, yes, maybe she was a tad overprotective, but that was her job.

"Buddy, we're doing fine, aren't we?" Claire leaned forward in her rickety wooden chair that'd been in her family for generations and had seen better days. Her whole house had seen better days. "I mean, it's not near as crazy as before, right? It's okay."

Before—when he'd been undergoing treatment. Before her life had fallen apart and the center of her world—her son—had nearly died. Not just once, but twice. Midnight trips to the hospital. Long stays while they fought to get his immune system sorted out. Weeks on end of never sleeping in their own beds.

"At least we're home more." She glanced around the kitchen. It was a mess. So were the family room and bedrooms. Adam was still being homeschooled. Until his immune system got back up to normal levels, it was better for him. Honestly, though, she liked him at home. Her life was chaotic. Dogs in the morning, each of whom needed to be taken out and exercised individually, then homeschooling, something she'd thought would be easy but had turned out to be hard, then back to work with the dogs, the office work in the afternoon because her "job" was to place the dogs in her care, and then work at her *other* job: graphic artist. Then it was back to work with Adam, then dinner, then bed, rinse, repeat. Unless there was a doctor's appointment—

"Mom?"

She'd been so lost in thought she hadn't even realized her son had spoken, and whatever it was he'd said must have been pretty important judging by the seriousness in his eyes.

"I'm sorry, bud. What did you say?"

She held back a chuckle when he said, "Jeez, were you even listening?" as a teenager would have said. Too much television.

She didn't bother trying to conceal her guilt. "Nope."

He released an exaggerated sigh that was so much like the old Adam that she smiled.

"I worry about you, Mommy. You're doing too much. There's all that paperwork about Dad.

The dogs. Me. I'm not a little boy anymore. I can take care of myself."

The paperwork for Dad. She was part of a lawsuit against the makers of the vaccine that'd made Marcus so sick. Yes, she admitted, Adam was right. That was a lot of work, too. But he was wrong about one thing. He was still a little boy. He might have seen more in this past year—friends dying, his mom's grieving, the harsh realities of life—than most people saw in a lifetime, but he would always be her little man. Always.

"Don't worry about me." She touched his chin. "I'm doing just fine."

"That's what every parent says until they drop dead from a heart attack."

The words were uttered so seriously and so matter-of-factly that she ended up smiling.

"I'm taking care of myself." Okay, so maybe she wasn't. She needed more sleep. Truth be told, she always felt so tired. And she would love some time for herself just as Adam suggested. To know that the dogs were taken care of and Adam looked after so she could escape into town to do a little window-shopping. All things she could hypothetically do right now, except she never did.

"All right." She sighed deeply. "I'll tell you what. When Dr. McCall comes over tomorrow morning I'll let him take care of the dogs for me. You can stay with me and help and I'll run into town for some errands."

Her son's whole face lit up and only in that moment did she truly understand just how much he'd been fretting over her.

"He said to call him Ethan. And that sounds like a deal."

Yes, she admitted, he had said to call him that, but for some reason, it felt better—safer—to add the doctor title in front of his name. He was here temporarily, after all. She wasn't going to become friends with him. Well, okay, she'd be friendly, but that was it.

Yeah. Keep telling yourself that.

Chapter Six

He slept more soundly than he had in months—
at least at first. But then, almost as if his sub-
conscious sensed the rising sun, the nightmares
began.

Trevor lay on the ground.

Fire.

BOOM.

He'd shot up, and then as his heart settled into
his chest, slipped from bed, walking over to the
row of windows that overlooked the old hay
barn and wondering, not for the first time, what
he was going to do. He wanted to train dogs. He
knew that, but he didn't want to give up being

a vet. He hated being a burden almost as much as he hated the nightmares that haunted him.

Focus.

The word had become his mantra. He had the entire upstairs portion—no little space as Colt's wife had made it sound. The roofline made for shorter walls to his right and left, but dormers had been placed at regular intervals, allowing light to spill in. It was bare. Nothing more than a space that echoed back the sound of his boots against the hardwood floor, but it felt like a mansion compared to his cramped quarters overseas.

He held up his hand, noticed it still trembled and forced himself to concentrate on the view outside. The sun had just started to peek over the horizon to his right. It cast a glow over the pastures and roofs and tops of trees, as if an artist had spilled a bucket of pink paint over one side of the canvas. If ever a place should soothe his nerves, this would be it, and yet he'd still had that terrible nightmare. Still felt the familiar edge of anxiety. Why? He wasn't worried about his new job, if one could call it that, because he recognized charity when he saw it, although in this instance it wasn't directed at him. They were trying to help Claire and her son. Well, okay. He could live with that, and he could play along. He could palpate a uterus with the best of them, and depending on the breed of horse, he could supervise a breeding. Thoroughbreds had to be live covered, meaning the stallion had to breed the mare naturally. Either way—AI or live cover—he could do that kind of work in his sleep.

He just wondered why he didn't get on with his life.

What he needed to do was start figuring out where he wanted to settle down, and which type of work he wanted to do: go to work as a city veterinarian and deal with Fido and his well-meaning but clueless owner? Or train dogs? The wise choice would be to do both, but the odds of doing both jobs well would be slim to nil. He should focus on finding a real job, maybe at a big horse-racing farm. He liked Reynolds Ranch. It would be great to find another place just like it.

Downstairs a horse nickered. He wondered who fed them and at what time. Maybe he could help out, because, damn it, he needed to be busy. His hands refused to stop shaking and he felt the familiar buzz of anxiety deep in the pit of his stomach where he knew it would slowly begin to unfurl as it did every morning until…

He wasn't going to let that happen. Not today, he thought, pulling on an old pair of jeans with a hole in the knee and a green button-down shirt, long-sleeved because he suspected it would be chilly outside. What he needed was work. Hard work. Only that would soothe the demons that haunted his soul.

He shot toward the front door. He had to keep

moving. His hand settled on the brass door handle, pushed, but despite the place being new, it liked to stick. He had to rattle it a few times to get it open, and when he did he paused for a moment on the covered landing, inhaling deeply. It was the smell of it all that soothed him like nothing else, he admitted. The air was fresh here, scented by dew and earth and freshly mown grass—the unmistakable smell of small town USA. It acted like a balm.

You can do this.

Colt must have heard him struggle with the door because he didn't seem surprised to see him. "Did I wake you?"

The man stood in the middle of the barn, tossing a flake he'd pulled from a giant feed cart to one of the horses. And what an animal it was. Today the feed doors were open and every single horse had stuffed their head through them, eyeing the human and his cart of hay as if they could somehow will Colt to feed them faster.

Each one of those heads was huge and yet beautiful, their coats glistening beneath the fluorescent lights in a way that spoke of excellent care.

"I was already up before these guys started nickering." He went up to the horse Colt was about to feed. "They're beautiful."

Colt used a hand to push the head of a dark bay back inside the feed door, then tossed the hay in afterward. "They should be, considering how much they cost."

Yesterday, Ethan had taken note of the nice-looking animal Colt's wife rode; this morning he realized she had a whole barn full of them.

"Something tells me your wife must be good at what she does." Down the row of stalls a horse began to bang his leg against a stall door. He moved forward. "Here. Let me help."

"One of the best in the world." He turned toward the horse protesting the complete ineptitude of his human caretakers. "Quit it!"

Silence. Colt smiled, shook his head, "Happens every morning." He pointed to the gallon-sized freezer bags housed in the cart, too. "You can give them their grain. Each horse has a packet with their name on it. Just match the packet to the name on the door."

Easy enough. "I take it your wife competes?" It wasn't just grain, he noted, inhaling the sweet scent of oats and molasses. It was grain and some kind of powder, vitamins no doubt, but it was a simple task to open the stall door and pour the baggies in a bright red bucket. In fact, it was just the sort of task he needed. Busywork.

"She just won a big grand prix back East. You should have seen it." Colt tossed another flake, then moved on to the next horse. "We pull into this big, elite show grounds with my Rodeo Misfits rig. Everyone on the 'circuit'—" he made air quotes with his fingers "—has these fancy buses. We pull up in my old rodeo rig and out comes Natalie and her horse. Of course, everyone knows who she is. They just hadn't seen her in a while, and they sure weren't expecting her to show up in a cattle trailer."

"Did her own rig break down or something?" He stepped back to admire the animal he'd just fed. The horse was huge. His whole opinion of the Reynoldses and their operation shifted. He'd assumed they were a local horse place and Natalie someone who gave lessons, but as they worked their way down the row, what he saw convinced him each one of the animals was world-caliber—not just one or two, but the whole barn.

"Something like that." Colt shrugged. "But these days she can afford what she wants. She's in the process of deciding what she wants to purchase." They'd reached the end of the row, Colt having already fed the other side, and so he turned to face Ethan while the horses quietly munched. "She was in a bad wreck almost two years ago. Nearly died. She was out of the business for a while… Hell, she stopped riding, but then she hooked up with me and all that… changed." He smiled and Ethan could tell Colt looked back on happy memories. "These days she's right back where she left off. Got a waiting list of clients and a bunch of talented horses in the barn, including that stallion over there." He nodded to the other side of the aisle, the black stallion Ethan hadn't fed yet. "We're thinking that guy over there might just win her a gold medal one day soon."

He walked toward the animal in question, a beautiful horse with small ears and a sculpted-looking head. "He's magnificent."

Colt nodded. "And easy to handle. Natalie already called the owner last night and told her our news. Honestly, you couldn't have come along at a better time. My sister needs a break with those dogs and we're about ready to hit the road pretty hard and so your arrival seems like a gift from God, as long as you don't mind a little hard work."

Work? It was the only thing that seemed to calm him down, which was why he didn't understand his inability to focus on the future. He should be out there finding a permanent job, not playing houseguest at a horse farm.

"I'll stick around until you find someone more permanent. It won't take me long to retrain Thor, and I don't want to be a burden."

"You won't be a burden," Colt said as they finished up. "And we'd love to discuss making this permanent. Natalie and I were talking and you've already been a big help, advising us on what equipment to buy last night. In fact, we were hoping you might stick around. There's a real need for a veterinarian in these parts. The closest vet is a friend of ours, but she's all the way in town. We're sure the ranchers out here would appreciate your presence. But, hell, I don't want to scare you with our big plans. Why don't I bring you over to my sister's place? You can get started with Thor."

Permanent? He wasn't ready to make a commitment like that. Not now. Maybe not ever.

His hands started to tingle. He stared down at them for a moment before saying, "Actually, if it's all the same to you, I think I'd rather walk."

THE SOUND OF dogs barking penetrated her consciousness, a little at first. Claire incorporated the sound into a dream where she was being chased by a pack of… Something. She sat up in bed.

Kennels.

The sound came from outside. The dogs were barking.

She crawled out of bed, the sheets clawing at her legs as if they were the paws of her phantom dogs. A quick glance out the window and she saw why they barked. A lonely-looking cowboy walked up the driveway.

Ethan.

She didn't know why her heart quickened.

Perhaps it was the remnant of her dream. Then again, her body always seemed to react whenever he was near. She might as well admit that.

"I don't have time for this."

She snatched the curtains closed, before he could see her, before he could spy her standing there in her white cotton nightgown that looked as if it belonged on a woman triple her age. At least, that's what it suddenly seemed like to her.

What was he doing here? And so early. A quick glance at her cell phone made her blanch because it wasn't that early at all. Eight o'clock—and the dogs hadn't been fed yet.

"Crap."

She grabbed the first thing she found—a pair of jeans and a bright orange T-shirt with *San Francisco* across the front. She barely glanced at her reflection in the mirror, just pulled her hair back off her face and shot out her bedroom door. No doubt Adam was sleeping, but she ducked her head in the room to make sure.

It'd been a while since she'd felt the familiar fear, the one that robbed her of breath as she crept to his bed and examined her son. *Was he still breathing?*

He was. But his skin was flushed and she knew with a mother's intuition that he was sick. She'd known it last night when he'd gotten irritable just before dinner. And then later when she'd ordered him to bed. She seen it in his glassy eyes and his flushed cheeks, too. Fever.

"Crap," she muttered again. She'd let him sleep, then check his temperature when she came back in from feeding the dogs.

But her feet were heavy when she opened her front door. Not just with fear, but with exhaustion and sadness and a growing sense of frustration.

Would it never end?

Lord, how she longed to be like a normal mother. A mom that had nothing more to worry about than getting her son to school on time and making sure his homework was done. There were days when worrying about Adam made her physically ill.

The sun nearly blinded her when the door swung wide. That's why she didn't see him standing there, not at first, his tall frame outlined by light. He wore a pair of jeans that looked as if they'd seen better days and a dark green shirt that probably matched his eyes. She didn't know. She was too afraid to look into them.

"You look like hell."

Her gaze shot to his. "Thanks."

"Not that you could ever look bad." Her eyes had adjusted enough that she could spot the consternation on his face. "I mean, I've always thought you were pretty."

Despite telling herself that it didn't matter, his words made her cheeks redden.

"You just look, I don't know, tired."

Beneath the brim of his cowboy hat she spotted embarrassment in his eyes. Funny, she felt just as self-conscious all of sudden.

"Long night with Adam," she admitted.

The embarrassment turned immediately to concern. "Is he okay?"

Would he ever be okay? Would their lives ever be able to go back to normal? Would there be a day when she could drop her guard and look to the future without worry or fear?

She took a deep breath. One day at a time.

"He's spiking a fever—I can tell." She slipped out the door and into the morning sunshine because she didn't want Adam to overhear their conversation. "He keeps talking about going into town for ice cream, but it's all just a front. He's getting sick and both of us know it."

"Isn't that dangerous?"

She nodded. "It can be. His immune system still isn't back to normal. Anytime he becomes ill there could be complications. I just have to keep an eye on him."

She shouldn't have taken him into town yesterday, but he'd begged her, and to be honest, she couldn't keep him locked up forever. The doctors had told her to just make sure he didn't come into contact with sick people. She made sure he washed his hands. She avoided restaurants and other places where a lot of people congregated. Still, there was only so much she could do.

"I bet you didn't get any sleep last night."

"I got enough."

The dogs had seen her. Their barking had changed from a warning to a whine. All except Thor. Once again the dog lay curled up in a ball right outside his loafing shed.

Ethan must have followed her gaze. "I'd like to work with him just as soon as he's finished eating."

"He's probably not hungry."

She kept the dog supplies in a shed she kept latched with a brass snap to keep the critters out of it. Damn raccoons were as clever as a human sometimes, and she would swear they checked that lock every night. Inside the room were barrels of dog food, the high performance kind that cost an arm and a leg and that she had to order from the feed store.

"You can fill bowls while I start scraping."

"How much do you feed?"

"A scoop per dog." She pointed to the white plastic mixing cup. "But if their bowl is already full, I just top it off."

They went to work, and to be honest, it felt good. Being busy took her mind off Adam inside the house and the obsessive need she felt to go back, to check his temperature again, but she couldn't do that. If he was sick, his best bet was rest, not an overanxious mom poking and prodding him every ten minutes.

It didn't take Ethan long to feed. She could hear him talking to the dogs as he went in and out of their kennels. She'd written their names on the outside just for that reason. In case she was suddenly called out of town—like back to Children's Hospital.

Don't think about it.

When he finished he caught up to her. They worked side by side then, Claire trying not to feel self-conscious while standing next to him. His hands weren't shaking this morning, and he seemed far more relaxed. The only time that changed was when they got to Janus. He tensed up then. She could see it in the way his hands gripped the shovel and the way the line of his jaw hardened.

"What are you working on with Thor today?"

She asked the question more as a way of distracting him than any real desire to engage in small talk. She couldn't stop herself from diving in. She hated seeing someone in pain, and Ethan very definitely had a hard time being around his buddy's dog.

He took a deep breath. "Probably keeping his gaze focused on me."

He scratched the dog on the chin one last time before straightening, the two of them finishing up together. When they were done she showed him where to wash up. She had an industrial-sized sink off the back of the shed, one she used to give the dogs their beauty treatments before heading off to a new home, and it was peaceful out back, a thick grove of oak trees just a few feet away. She'd had Colt help her install a gate, one constructed out of old oak so that it blended with the trees behind, and that led to a path where she liked to walk along the nearby creek.

"I'm just going to go check on Adam."

He nodded, but he seemed lost in thought as she quickly slipped away. Adam still slept, and while he didn't feel hot, that didn't reassure her. Her little man tried so hard to be brave.

Ethan was right where she'd left him, or near

enough. He rested his arms against a fence post, staring out into the woods. Their gazes met and she saw something in the depths of his eyes that reminded her of the first day they'd met.

"How is he?"

"Still sleeping."

He glanced back toward the kennels. "He's going to hate missing out on my training session with Thor."

She nodded. "Maybe you could do it later?"

She thought he might say no, would bet her best pair of boots that he thought about it, but instead he said, "Why not?" He smiled, but it was brief, like a patch of sunlight that had escaped from between storm clouds. "I don't have anything better to do."

He'd gone back to looking lost again, and sad, and maybe even tense, especially when his gaze hooked on the kennel that belonged to Janus. It prompted her to head toward the gate a few feet away, and to her walking path. Her way of escaping reality, at least for a few minutes. Her balm for the soul because she'd noticed nothing soothed her more than the sweet smell of Mother Nature. Perhaps it would work for Ethan, too.

"Come on. Let's walk."

He seemed surprised by her invite, but she smiled, trying to reassure him without words. They were two peas in a pod. He grieved over the loss of his buddy and she grieved over the loss of her son's childhood.

He seemed to nod, as if somehow reading her mind, then stepped forward.

"He was a good friend, wasn't he?" She asked the question as she opened the gate, stepping aside so he could join her. She had a perfect view of his face and so she saw the corners of his eyes flex, as if he fought to keep from revealing too much.

"The best."

They walked in silence for a moment, Claire

feeling her back pocket to ensure she had her cell phone. They had pretty good service out here thanks to a cell tower on the nearby hills. Adam could call her if he needed her. They would be within shouting distance, too, the house visible from her favorite spot through a thick grove of oak trees.

"Did you know him long?"

"Not too long. A few years, but we used to joke that in combat years, it was a lifetime."

Maybe it was her exhaustion, or maybe it was her inability to mind her own business, but for some reason she found herself pushing for answers. "You were there with him, weren't you? When it happened, I mean."

It was just a simple question, one she suspected she already knew the answer to, so she would never have demanded an answer. They'd reached her favorite spot. An old, fallen tree lay alongside the creek, the bark worn away where she and Adam sat all the time. Her footfalls had long since worn a path around it and she followed the path now, urging him to sit next to her as the water gurgled by. Few things seemed to settle a human soul like the sound of running water and the smell of a forest. It was as if something primordial kicked in, a deep-rooted sense of belonging that acted as a balm to the rush of life.

"I was with him," he said as he sat down beside her.

That was all she'd been curious about and so she didn't push him for more. She watched a leaf slide by on the soft current that pushed the creek toward the ocean. She hoped the smell of wet earth and dank vegetation soothed him as it always had her.

"We'd just left base."

She glanced at him quickly because this she hadn't expected. "It's okay. You don't have to talk about it if you don't want to."

He stuck his hands in his pockets and she

knew he'd begun to shake again. "No. That's all right. I think maybe I should."

Still, he didn't immediately launch into the tale and for a moment she wondered if he'd changed his mind.

"We were on our way home. We'd made it, both of us, to the end. We were leaving, and when we reached stateside, we were going to open up a training business.

"That morning, Trev left ahead of me to secure our ride. I had some dogs in my care, so I had to wrap a few things up, but I wasn't that far behind."

She could tell the next part would be hard, felt the urge to take his hand in her own, the desire so strong, her empathy so keen, she almost told him to stop, that she didn't want to hear. Instead, she tightened her own hands into fists and simply listened.

"He was gone maybe ten minutes, couldn't have been more than that, when it started.

Boom! One moment sunshine and sky, the next dirt and broken glass. And then another boom and another. We were under attack."

He rubbed his arms absently and she realized that's where the scars came from, the ones she'd noticed the day he'd arrived. They were covered by the dark green shirt he wore, but he still touched them.

"It doesn't register at first when something like that happens, you know?" He turned and met her gaze and her heart broke into a million pieces at just the look in his eyes. Yes, she'd known he'd lost his friend, but it wasn't until that moment that she realized just how badly it'd affected him. "It felt like a dream. The psychologists say it's a natural reaction to trauma, some sort of mental self-defense. At first I thought it was just a nightmare, that we couldn't really be under attack, and so I just sat there."

She knew all too well that sense of denial. She'd felt the same thing when she'd realized there was no hope for Marcus. That he was going to die. Time and again she'd wake up thinking it was all a bad dream only to roll over and spy the empty bed next to her and realize that Marcus really was in the hospital and that he really wasn't going to come home.

"And suddenly it hits you that it *is* happening and that you have to do something."

His gaze sharpened. "All I could think about was Trevor. And Janus. They were up ahead of me and I knew from experience they'd bear the brunt of the attack."

A part of her didn't want to hear the rest. Another part knew he needed to get it out.

"I jumped out. I don't even remember the explosion next to me, but fragments hit my arms. I just remember the sting of something, but I didn't care. I grabbed my sidearm and took off only when I looked ahead—"

She found herself reaching for his hand and clutching it despite telling herself not to touch him. "It's okay." She squeezed. "You don't have to keep going. I can imagine what you saw." It was her worst fear come to life—being in the wrong place at the wrong time. When Marcus had been overseas she'd prayed every day he'd make it home. She prayed the same thing for her brothers. The irony was that Marcus had made it home, but he'd been terribly ill from the day he stepped stateside. She'd changed her prayer then. She wanted her brothers to come home healthy and strong.

He'd turned away from her, his face in profile. It was like watching a movie play across his face, one where she could see the actors, but not listen to the lines. She didn't need to hear them, though. She could tell he recalled the scene he'd stumbled upon. Knew he remembered finding his friend's body. That he tried to shut it out, but that he couldn't.

Please, God, keep Chance safe these last few months.

She clutched his hand harder.

"Sometimes I can still smell it. Burnt rubber. Spilled fuel. Gunpowder. And…other things. It was total chaos. But just as suddenly as it started, it stopped. There were medics on scene, but I knew I couldn't help Trev. I needed to let the medics do their thing." She saw his eyes fill with tears, felt his fingers clutch her own. "But I could help Janus, and so I did, yet some days I wonder if I shouldn't have at least tried to help Trev."

She let go of his hand, touched his chin, asking without words for him to turn back to her again. He did so reluctantly, but that was okay. She needed him to hear her words.

"Some memories will always be a part of us. The trick is to learn to let them go. Or to put them in a place where they can no longer hurt us." She could tell he barely heard her. "You need to replace those bad memories with good

ones. In time those good memories will out-
number the bad."

He huffed sarcastically. "Good ones?"

She nodded.

"And where do I find those?"

He seemed so lost, so completely adrift in a
sea of fear and sadness and self-rebuke that she
did the unthinkable. She leaned into him, her
lips brushing his own, whispering the words,
"You can start right here," kissing him before
she could think better of it.

And God help her, it felt right.

Chapter Seven

She was his anchor in a storm-tossed sea of memories, Ethan thought. Her lips were soft and warm and all he wanted to do was stay right there, to absorb her heat and her scent and the earthy goodness that was her.

She pulled back. He let her go, but he didn't allow her to pull away entirely. He cupped the back of her head with his hands, rested her forehead against his own and peered into green eyes that seemed both troubled and terrified.

"I'm sorry." She blinked. "That was out of line. I didn't mean to—"

"Shh." His thumb slid forward, the edge of it

brushing her lips. So soft. So plump. So tempting. He didn't know what had just happened. He only knew that having her near, holding her like this, peering into her eyes—it all somehow righted his world.

Her eyes closed and she bowed her head. He let her go, inhaling deeply, wondering if this was why he'd driven all those miles. If somehow he'd known she'd be a balm to his soul.

"I should get back. Adam—"

How long had they been sitting there? Five minutes? Ten? He couldn't recall, but he knew she was right. She had a son. A little boy who had battles of his own to wage.

"I'll walk you back."

He grabbed her hand, and as he helped her up, he wondered what she'd do if he tugged her to him. Just as quickly as the idea had come, he let it go. She'd kissed him out of kindness. Even as messed up as he was, he could see that.

"Thank you," he said.

She glanced up sharply. "For what?"

"For listening."

She searched his eyes for something—what, he didn't know. "Anytime."

Once again, he noticed the beauty of her eyes. It wasn't just their color. It was everything in them. Kindness. Strength. And a sweetness of spirit that made him wonder what it would be like to know her—truly know her. He shook his head at such a thought. They were two human beings brought together by tragedy, nothing more.

He had to force his thoughts away from her, and it was hard, but at least he no longer felt like a soldier out on a battlefield, scared, wanting to run, to get away from it all. He could breathe now. It brought everything into focus: The way light dappled the ground in front of them. The sound of the creek as it moved forward. The smell of dried oak leaves and wild sage. All of it reminded him of happier times. Days from his childhood when he'd gone camping, back when the biggest problem he'd had was how to carry his fishing pole and tackle box and cooler all in one trip so he could beat the other boys to the best spot on the river.

"Did you drive over?" she asked.

They'd reached the gate. "No. I walked."

She nodded. "Do you need a lift back? We could wait until Adam is up."

"No." His gaze caught on her lips, and it shocked him how much he wanted to pull her to him, and how badly he longed to kiss her again, and if they were alone in her house with her son asleep in bed… "I can walk back after I work with Thor."

Her eyes widened a bit and he could tell she'd forgotten about him working with Thor. He wondered for a moment if she wanted him to leave. If maybe she regretted their kiss, but try as he might, he couldn't read her eyes.

"Adam's going to want to watch you."

"You can call me back over once he's up."

"No. I should wake him up now. If he sleeps too long I'll never get him to bed at a decent hour tonight."

"Then I'll wait. He can watch from a window."

"There are leashes and treats in the feed room."

"I know. I saw."

She looked as if she wanted to say something more. He waited, and for the first time, held his breath over something not related to Trevor and the horrors of his past. But whatever it was she wanted to say, she lost her nerve.

"I'll be right back."

SHE'D KISSED HIM.

Stupid, stupid, stupid.

It wasn't as if she didn't have enough problems of her own. She didn't need to take on the troubles of a near stranger, too.

"Rise and shine, kiddo." She sat on the edge of Adam's bed. If ever she needed a reminder of all the reasons why she should steer clear of Ethan, this was it, she told herself. Her son's cheeks were still flushed, so much so that she reached out and touched them.

Hot. She drew back her hand as if stung. "No."

She ran for the thermometer, cursing herself the whole time. She should have been attending to her son, not kissing Ethan.

"Hey, buddy," she said, sitting back down on the edge of the bed and gently shaking him. "I need to take your temperature." She nudged him awake, and he slowly blinked the sleep from his eyes, his cheeks stained red.

His gaze snagged on her own. She saw his eyes move around the room as if trying to reason out if he was awake or if this was a dream. "Don't feel well."

It took every ounce of her willpower to force a

smile on her face. Inside, though, she fell apart. Should she call the doctor? They had warned her this might happen. He'd been doing so well, though. She'd been meticulous about keeping him away from sick people and disinfecting his hands whenever he went out.

"Let's take your temperature." First things first. Maybe she was wrong. Maybe she just imagined the heat of his body.

He was so sick, though—fever or no—all he did was nod his head, and in some ways, that scared her even more. Even before his diagnosis he'd always been her tough kid. The one that had to be practically missing a limb before he slowed down. The whole time they'd been undergoing treatment it'd been the same way. He had been terribly sick once before, but that'd been in the hospital. It'd been a long forty-eight hours while they waited for his temperature to drop. The longest hours of her life, but she'd had a full staff of professionals around her to assuage her fears. This time she'd be on her own.

She trembled as she checked the digital thermometer, but she had herself in control when she went back into Adam's room. If he saw her panic he'd start to fret and if he started to fret she would fall apart.

It's just a little bug, she told herself. *He'll be fine.* "Open up," she told him.

Probably just a cold.

But his immune system wasn't 100 percent. They were optimistic about having cured the leukemia, but that battle had left her son more vulnerable to even a simple cold bug.

Beeeeep.

She didn't want to look. She really didn't, not when she already knew the answer. She forced herself to read the numbers anyway.

One hundred and three.

"Son of a—"

Even as sick as he was, Adam's eyes popped open. "Is it bad?"

Her son, the boy who didn't fear anything, looked terrified now. "Not too high," she lied. "I'm going to give you some medicine, then call the doctor."

"Am I going to the hospital again?"

"No." She forced a smile. "Of course not. Dr. Jones warned me this might happen. He told me to check in with him if it did. You'll be fine."

Would he? Would he really be fine? And if he wasn't, could she face another loss? This past year she'd asked herself that question at least a million times and she always came up with the same answer.

No.

She would not be fine. She would fall apart, and she wasn't certain she could put the pieces back together again.

She glanced outside. Ethan had Thor out. She'd need to tell him. But first, she had to call the doctor.

WHAT WAS TAKING so long?

Adam must have been awake, he reasoned. She was probably helping him get dressed. Or getting him breakfast. Or helping him to find a missing shoe. But there were no little boy noises coming from the house. No slammed cabinets and no heavy footsteps. Just near quiet.

He touched Thor's head. The dog looked up at him. He might not be able to hear, but there was nothing wrong with his sight and the dog was already used to looking for hand signals. In just five minutes he was making progress on having Thor keep constant eye contact, something the dog wasn't used to doing since canines relied on their ears just as much as their eyesight and smell. It filled him with a self-satisfaction that he'd made even that little bit of progress in such a short amount of time.

Still nothing from inside the house.

He tugged on the leash. This, too, Thor understood. The difference would be to teach Thor to keep his eyes on his handler instead of perpetually looking around and being on alert. He needed to undo Thor's training to a certain degree and so he stopped, tapping the dog on the top of the head so he and Thor made eye contact, then praised him and set off again.

Claire.

She had kissed him out of kindness. He wasn't so messed up in the head that he didn't recognize pity when it kissed him, but the fact that he'd broken down in front of her didn't help his self-esteem. It was at an all new low.

The front door slammed. He turned.

"Adam won't be joining you."

Her eyes were rimmed with red—as if she'd

recently cried, but gotten herself under control before coming to see him. "What's the matter?"

"He has a fever."

He knew enough about Adam's illness to recognize what a serious issue that was. "Is there anything I can do?"

She shook her head. "I have to go back inside. I'm waiting for a call back from the doctor."

He nodded. She took a few steps back, then waved goodbye. Something in her eyes before she'd turned away made him feel like a jerk for worrying about his own troubles when she clearly had so much more to deal with than he did.

You're alive, buddy. Quit dwelling on the past.

The voice was Trevor's and it caused Ethan's eyes to close. Instantly an image of his friend rose up before him. The smart-ass smile. The cocky grin. The look of impatience when Ethan didn't rush right into something. That was why they'd gotten along so well. Ethan prided himself on being cautious. Trevor liked to rush right in and get things done.

When he opened his eyes, he found himself facing the kennels, Janus staring back at him.

Trevor would have told him to get off his ass and stop feeling sorry for himself. There were other things he could be doing with his time; like helping Claire, a woman who had clearly reached the end of her rope, yet still had a sweetness of spirit that led her to reach out to others in need.

He would do the same.

He put Thor away, giving the dog a pat on the head before releasing him, then headed toward her front door before he could think better of it and knocked on it. He heard her footsteps, quick and businesslike, before the door swung wide. Claire was just as stressed in appearance as she'd been two minutes earlier.

"What's up?" she asked, glancing past him as

if she might glean a clue as to why he suddenly knocked on her door.

"I'm going to cook you breakfast."

Her face registered puzzlement. "But I'm not hungry."

"You will be," he said, sliding past her. He might be many things, messed up in the head being one of them, but he was a hell of a cook.

"But, I might have to leave for the hospital in a few minutes."

"Then I'll finish cooking breakfast, then stay here and keep an eye on the place."

She stood by the door, fingers still on the handle, her green eyes as worn and tired as woman triple her age and his heart broke for her. Even though she had family less than a mile away, he had a feeling she tried to do most of it alone.

"Adam is sick and I'm not sure—"

"Shh." He came forward, pressing a hand against her lips, and for the first time in weeks felt tasked with a purpose. "I'm going to stay."

Chapter Eight

It took forever for the doctor to call back. Claire didn't know what stressed her out more: waiting for her phone to ring, or the man who cooked breakfast in her kitchen.

Adam stirred in his bed. She had parked herself next to him, watching, calling herself obsessive at least a million times, but not really caring. Something might change. She might need to be there for him. Bathroom. Drink of water. Medicine. She would always have to be there for him, which was why the man in the kitchen—

"What smells good?"

She glanced at the bed in surprise. Her son's eyes, glassy and red from fever, peered up at her in curiosity.

"It's Ethan. He's cooking us breakfast." And all right. It did smell good. No. It smelled delicious.

Adam's eyes closed.

"Do you want some?"

Adam gave a sleepy nod, one that buoyed Claire's spirits because if he was hungry it couldn't be that bad. At least that was what she told herself as she got up from the chair and headed toward Ethan. She drew up short at what she saw. Ethan stood there, the sleeves of his green shirt rolled up to his elbows, his scars barely visible, an apron of hers tied around his waist, one with the words *Hot Mama* on the front. On the counter next to him sat a pile of pancakes even though she couldn't remember ever buying the mix. And he'd clearly found the package of bacon in her refrigerator because that was the smell wafting through the house and causing her stomach to growl.

"Adam is hungry."

He turned toward her.

She'd kissed him.

Best not to dwell on that, she told herself. "I thought I'd bring him a plate of food."

"I have something just for him."

He bent, opening the oven beneath the stove, and removed a plate. Next he fished a piece of bacon out of the pan, then picked up a smaller, narrower pot, Claire watching as he poured syrup over everything.

"Here you go."

On the plate was a pig, complete with a pig nose and ears, and chocolate chips for nostrils. He'd somehow made it look as if that pig was smiling.

She didn't know why the sight made her heart flip over, but it did.

"Tell him to eat up. That whole 'starve a fever

and feed a cold' thing is an old wives' tale. He needs nutrients to help him fight off whatever's attacking him."

And then suddenly she wanted to cry. He cared. He wanted to help. To reassure her.

"Thanks."

He waved his spatula. "You're going to eat, too."

"I will, after Adam."

That must have satisfied him because he nodded once again, then went back to making his bacon. She stared down at the plate and found herself wishing Marcus was still alive with a ferociousness that took her aback. Ethan reminded her of him, she realized. He used to make her breakfast, too.

It took all her effort to slip on a smile, though it felt as false as an infomercial as she gently nudged Adam awake again. "Want some food?"

Her son stared up at her through eyes that were so much like Marcus's that it kicked her in the gut. They might be feverish and red, but those were Marcus's long lashes. Or maybe it was the shape of his eyes or the line of his brows. Something about Adam's face reminded her of her lost husband to the point that she had to clutch the plate to keep from dropping it.

"Come on." She used as chipper a voice as possible. "At least have a few bites."

Though he'd expressed interest in it earlier, she could tell her son wasn't really hungry. She could also tell he didn't want to displease her. It was one thing she'd noticed about him. He always tried to put a brave face on things—for her. It broke her heart.

He slowly shifted until he was sitting up. It was just lack of sleep that made her so shaky. That and the fact that she'd kissed Ethan. Exhaustion had eroded her common sense.

"Do you see what he made you?" she asked with false brightness as she helped him sit up. "It's a pig."

He tried to smile, but it was obvious it took all his effort just to sit up. Whatever it was that attacked his immune system it had managed to physically drain him. When he sat up she didn't even bother to hand him a fork.

"And he must have made it all from scratch." She cut off a bite. "Just have a little bit, then you can go back to sleep."

He obediently opened his mouth and she tried not to fret as she watched him eat. She'd been up half the night running through various scenarios. What she would do if his fever spiked. What she would say to the doctor when he called back. Who she would call if she needed to leave the ranch. Around and around her thoughts had tumbled until, suddenly, it was daybreak and Ethan had been walking up her driveway.

"N'more."

Her fork froze halfway. He'd held up a hand and she hadn't even noticed it. When she glanced at the plate it was to note he'd eaten hardly anything at all.

"Just a little more."

He shook his head, sank down and rolled over on his side, and she just stared, her spirits sinking even further. Days like today it was hard to keep her chin up. She tried to maintain a positive attitude, knew that if Adam saw her lose her cool it would upset him, maybe even cause him to panic, and right now she needed him happy, or as happy as a sick child could be. She refused to distract him with her own mental breakdowns.

But her body quaked as she stood and silently left the room. Her lip quivered. She knew she was on the verge of tears. She stared down at the plate in her hand. The last thing she wanted was for Ethan to see her red-rimmed eyes, because sure as certain she was about to bawl her eyes out.

Dumb, dumb, dumb.

She slipped into her bedroom, swung the door closed behind her and set the plate down on her nightstand. Ironically, though, the tears wouldn't come. It was as if there was so much sorrow inside her that it dammed up her tear ducts to the point nothing could escape. Her stomach roiled, her mind churned, her heart broke for her son—but her eyes refused to let loose.

"You okay?"

She turned sharply, on the verge of telling Ethan to close the door again, but he didn't stand inside the room. He spoke through a crack, one that made her belatedly realize the door hadn't swung closed all the way.

"Fine."

She turned back around, took a deep breath, hoped he didn't hear the way her voice cracked. What a pair they were. Him mourning the loss of his friend. Her morning the loss of her happiness.

"You want to eat?"

Her gaze snagged on Adam's half-eaten food. "In a bit."

She took a deep breath, reminding herself that she would get through this. She would make it through tomorrow, too. And the next day after that. What choice did she have?

Ethan still stood on the other side of the door. "Come here."

She didn't want to. Crazy, really, considering she'd been the one to console him less than an hour before. She didn't think she could take his kindness, though. She needed to do this on her own—as she always did.

She opened the door and brushed past him. "I'm going to grab something to eat."

The words were a contradiction to what she'd just said, but Claire didn't care. She needed to say something, anything, to escape from him. No, she quickly amended. To escape from the urge to do exactly as he suggested; to sink into his arms and forget for the moment that she was the single mother of a very sick little boy.

"Claire." He called her name and she ignored it, turning toward the kitchen.

He intercepted her halfway there.

"I need to eat."

"No," he said. "You need a hug."

Funny how just a moment ago she couldn't cry to save her life, yet his words roused instant tears in her eyes. "Please don't."

"Don't what?"

She sucked in a breath, trying hard not to crumble because that was all it'd taken—one gentle call of her name, one random act of kindness, one offer of a shoulder to lean upon—for her to lose strength.

"Don't be kind to me because if you touch me I might crumble and if I crumble I don't know if I'll be able to put all the pieces back together again."

He stared down at her with a kindness that

melted her self-control. "If you crumble, I promise to help put you back together again."

He tugged her toward him. She tried to resist, but he wouldn't let her, and then the tears were coming. Soft tears because she didn't want Adam to hear. And then the tears turned into sobs. He muffled the sound with his shirt and a part of her worried that she was making a mess on the fabric, probably leaving mascara stains, but he kept on holding her.

A long time later she leaned back, sniffed, a part of her mortified that he'd seen her break down.

"Better?"

She nodded.

"Liar."

She nodded again. He smiled, a tender smile, one that made her whole body go still. Something flickered in his eyes, something that caused a warning to scream through her head.

Step away.

She didn't, God help her, she didn't, and so when he lowered his head toward her own, she didn't move then, either.

"Claire," he said softly.

Whether he closed that final distance or she did, she would never know. All she knew was the heat of his lips against her own and the feel of his body pressed up against her chest was the sweetest slice of heaven she'd had in a long, long time. It started as the softest of kisses, one meant to reassure her and comfort her. But then it changed, and she let it happen because, Lord, it'd been so long.

She'd forgotten about the way a body could tighten and tingle and warm with just a kiss. And so when those lips moved away and nuzzled her jaw and then the side of her neck, his teeth lightly nipping her, she let him do it. She even sighed when he cupped her breast. His other hand parted her shirt even more and she knew what he would do next. God help her, she welcomed his touch, her bra sliding over her sensitive skin until she was exposed to his view, but not for long. Oh, no. His mouth covered her and she thought she might lose it right then and there. How had she managed to forget the way it felt to have a man nip at her? Why hadn't she remembered how good it was, or how exciting, when that same man used his mouth to tease and taunt her? Her body had become a live wire, one that sizzled in his arms.

His hand shifted even lower. The sizzling turned into a burn. When he found her center it was all she could do not to cry out. She wilted. He pulled her to him and she let him carry her away and away and away.

Her knees gave out.

If he hadn't been holding her she would have fallen to the floor. But he held her while she spiraled around and around and around until she slowly, gently returned to Earth.

Her hands clutched his shirt. She hadn't even noticed.

What are you doing?

The words were her first coherent thought. This was neither the time nor the place to be doing something like that. Adam was right on the other side of the door, for goodness' sake.

What kind of parent was she?

She tried to slip away. His arms held her tight, his own head resting against the top of hers.

"It's okay," he said softly.

No. It wasn't okay. She had no business indulging in pleasure, not with her son so sick. She was the worst sort of parent.

"I need to check on Adam."

Chapter Nine

He played with fire.

Ethan rested his hands on the counter, staring at the granite surface. She was clearly at the end of her rope. Clearly vulnerable. Clearly in need of an escape, and he'd taken advantage of that fact. He shouldn't have done that.

Outside, the dogs started barking. He glanced up and out the window in time to spy a truck coming down the drive. Colt. Probably wondering what had happened to him. Thank goodness the man hadn't come a few minutes earlier.

He threw back his shoulders. He had no idea where Claire had gone, but he had a feeling she wouldn't want to greet her brother. Not until she composed herself.

The truck came to a stop near the kennels. Ethan headed out the side door.

"There you are," Colt said, a smile on his face. "I was thinking you might have gotten lost."

He forced a welcoming grin. "Nope. Just helping your sister out." His smile collapsed beneath the weight of his guilt for a second. "Adam isn't feeling well."

Colt's smile slipped off his face, too. "What's wrong?"

"He's got a fever. Pretty bad one, I guess." *And I just made your sister cry out in pleasure.* "I just made them breakfast, but Adam didn't eat hardly anything at all."

Colt nodded, heading quickly inside the house. Ethan headed toward the kennels. Fresh air. He needed more of it. Claire had probably heard him talking to her brother. She'd had time to compose herself, no doubt. If he was smart he'd start heading back to his new quarters, but he couldn't just leave her after kissing her like that. They should talk. He should apologize. Hell, he should go get his head examined—for more reasons than one.

Janus eyed him from his kennel. There were times, like now, when he missed his friend with an intensity that hurt. Physically hurt. It made his heart race, the tempo increasing until he found himself setting off in Janus's direction. The dog greeted him at the gate.

"Hey, buddy."

Janus ducked his head as if to say "hey" right back. Ethan scrubbed the dog on the top of the head before straightening again.

"Foos."

The dog instantly moved to Ethan's leg. He set off, waiting until he was in the clearing between the house and the kennels before ordering the dog to run. Janus shot off at a fast clip.

"Sitz."

The dog sat. Hard, and when he turned to face him, he had what could only be called a canine grin on his face. It brought a smile to Ethan's face.

"Missed this, have you, buddy?"

The dog had begun to pant, the excited kind of pant, eyes firmly fixed on him as he waited for the next command.

"Hier." The dog came at him. *"Blieb."* The dog stopped, and Ethan was suddenly struck by the difference between now and the last time he'd put a dog through his paces. He'd been on another continent. In a war zone. Nothing but desert all around him.

This was better. He took a deep breath and listened to the birds and the gentle rush of water in the nearby creek and the smell of the roses that grew along the edge of the house. This was much, *much* better.

"Impressive." He turned and found Colt watching him. "I've never seen them work before."

"Sitz," he told Janus before turning back to Colt.

"Why do you talk to them in German?" Colt asked. "I've always wondered."

"Because most of the pups come from overseas. They're taught German from a young age. It's just easier to keep using the commands in their native tongue rather than teach them a new language."

Colt nodded. "Makes sense."

Did he know what had happened? Had Claire told him? He didn't think so.

"Is everything okay in there?" Ethan asked.

Colt shrugged. "She's worried."

So she hadn't mentioned anything, not that he thought she really would. "Has she heard back from the doctor?"

"Actually, yes. He said this was all part of the process. We have to build Adam's immunity back up again, and unless he keeps spiking a really high fever, not to worry. So she's in there right now checking his temperature again and I'm sure she'll be obsessing over it all day."

Ethan didn't doubt it. He didn't blame her, either. This was her son. He had a serious illness.

"How bad was the cancer?"

Sadness entered Colt's eyes. "Right now? Not bad. They have it on the run. The problem is we won't know for sure if it's truly gone for a few more months yet. It's a wait-and-see kind of thing."

What a horrible stress to be under. And he'd gone and kissed her as if there was nothing wrong with the world. What a putz.

"Janus." He waited for the dog to look up at him, then motioned for him to run. The dog galloped off. *"Sitz."* He waited for the dog to sit before turning back to Colt. "What can I do to help?"

The man in front of him might wear a cowboy hat. He might seem like a tough as nails cowboy, but Ethan could see the concern in his eyes.

"Just do what you can around here. We could really use the help, what with my wife and I constantly gone and Claire off to the doctors at a moment's notice. I can't tell you how grateful we are that you showed up. It's like a godsend or something."

For the first time all morning Ethan felt less like a jerk, but only just a little. He still shouldn't have kissed her. What was he? In high school or something where he couldn't keep his hormones in check? "Done."

"She likes to think she can do it all herself."

"I've noticed."

"And she'll work herself right into ground."

"I'll make sure that doesn't happen, sir."

The formality of his address clearly caught Colt by surprise, but old habits died hard. "I'd appreciate that." He glanced back at the house. "Maybe you can split your time between here and my ranch. If you're okay with that," he added quickly.

"I've got all the time in the world."

Maybe he really was meant to be here. Maybe, for once, he was in the right place at the right time.

IT WAS THE longest two days of Claire's life. She hovered between rushing Adam to the hospital and calling his oncologist every five minutes. When, after a long seventy-two hours later, his fever finally broke, it was all Claire could do not to break down and cry. Again. More shocking was that she didn't want to call her brother with the news that Adam was better. No. The first person she wanted to tell was Ethan.

How bizarre was that?

She glanced out the window, because there he was. Outside. Working Thor. He'd been an incredible help the past few days. He split his time between working at her brother's place and walking down the road to help her with the dogs. He checked in with her every morning and every night, too, keeping his distance, even though all she wanted to do when she opened the door was invite him in and…

No. Not again. She would not be weak ever again.

"Mom. Can I go outside?" Adam stared up at her with wide, green eyes, a blanket wrapped around his shoulders. His Hawkman blanket. Its dark blue color made his skin appear paler than normal. Then again, he had been sick for three days.

"Oh, I don't know, hon. You just got out of bed for the first time an hour ago."

"I know." His green eyes implored. "But I'm better now. No more fever."

No more fever for now. It could come back. *Stop.*

She had to quit thinking like that. She needed to focus on the positives in her life. Adam had gotten over an illness, a first for him since they'd stopped treatment of his leukemia. He hadn't been rushed to a hospital. He hadn't spent days in the ER. Still, her baby boy was sick and it broke her heart. Comma-shaped smudges cupped the bottom of his eyes. They made the green stand out even more. He needed color.

He needed sun.

"Okay. For just a bit."

His whoop of joy filled her soul with happiness. She shouldn't be such a spoilsport, she told herself. She needed to let him go have some fun.

"Five minutes," she said, following him to his room where he quickly slipped on a pair of jeans.

He might have been deathly ill yesterday, but you wouldn't know it by the way he moved around, sliding one of his favorite comic book T-shirts over his head. He was out the door before she could tell him to brush his hair.

Let him go. Don't crowd him. He'll be fine.

She might have gone after him but her laptop chimed, and for a second she forgot about

Adam and his illness in her rush to get to her computer in time.

"Chance?" she said, smiling for the first time in days as her brother's face came into view.

"Hey, little sister, how's it going?"

Her brother looked tired, or maybe it was just the feed, or even the military uniform he wore. The pale colors enhanced the green of his eyes, but it made the exhaustion more evident by highlighting the smudges beneath his eyes.

"Better," she said. She'd sent him an email the other day telling him about Adam and how sick he was. She never had any idea when he would see things, but he must have gotten this one relatively quickly. "His fever broke last night."

His green eyes lit up. "That's good news."

His mouth moved before the words arrived. She'd never quite gotten used to the effect—not with her husband, not with Colt and not with Chance.

"It really is. He hasn't gotten over an illness

all on his own in over a year. The doctor said it's a good sign."

Dr. Pembra, the oncologist, had called at the crack of dawn, but she hadn't minded. In fact, she appreciated Children's Hospital and their staff more than she could put into words. Between Dr. Pembra and Dr. Jones she knew she had the best team possible.

"And that other matter? Is that still a problem?"

Damn her inability to keep things to herself. She'd been desperate to talk to someone about what had happened with Ethan, and what better way to do it than by pounding her keyboard like some kind of teenage blogger? She must have been really desperate, she thought, but who better than her brother overseas? Although not for long, she reminded herself. He'd be home soon.

"He's still here."

A black eyebrow lifted. The three siblings were all dark. All had fair skin. All had green eyes, although Chance's were more hazel than green. They took after their mother, and not a day went by that she didn't wish she was still alive.

"And is that a good thing or bad?"

The picture froze for a moment and she waited with bated breath to see if they would lose the connection, but in a flash the image caught up with itself.

"Actually, it's been a good thing. He's been a big help while Adam's been sick."

Chance nodded. "Colt tells me he's been a big help over at their place, too."

He'd talked to Colt? "You didn't tell him what I told you, did you?"

Chance smiled, the grin making his eyes light up in a way that seemed so very boyish despite the hell he'd been through overseas. One day some woman would fall for him hard. She just wasn't sure he'd reciprocate the feelings. The military was his life. Always had been and always would be. No ranch life for him.

"No, of course not," he answered. "I wasn't about to spread the news that my naughty little sister had gotten all hot and heavy with a houseguest while my sick nephew slept in his room."

"Oh, jeez." She covered her face with her hands.

She heard Chance laugh. "Hey. Relax. It's not like you had sex. And even if you had, everyone needs to blow off some steam once in a while."

No, but she'd enjoyed Ethan's touch just a little too much for comfort. "I'd rather not talk about it."

The lips moved before the words "Then why'd you tell me?" came through the tiny speaker on her laptop.

"That was a mistake."

"Nah." He shifted back in his seat, crossing his arms. A Gilly suit. That was what Chance called his outfit. "You needed someone to talk to about it."

He was probably right. She hadn't known what to think about her lapse in judgment, but it was clear by the twinkle in Chance's eyes that he thought it was funny. Heck, he might even approve.

"I'm fine about it now," she lied. "And it hasn't happened again."

"Maybe it should."

"And maybe it shouldn't."

Her brother knew her well enough that he knew when to let a matter drop. But just in case, she quickly launched into the latest happenings around the ranch. The last time they'd seen each other had been a month or so after Colt and Natalie had gotten married—a quickie marriage in their own backyard. They'd seen him for a day and she supposed she should be grateful for that.

"Hey, sis," he said as she was about to go get

Adam so the two could talk. "Don't forget to take care of yourself."

"I am doing that."

"No," he said. "I don't mean getting rest—I mean living life."

"Chance—"

"I mean it. Time for you to start relaxing and having fun."

He meant she should kiss Ethan again. "I do have fun." Just not that kind of fun.

But he ignored her. "Where's my nephew?"

She thought about pushing the matter, but the truth was she really wanted to escape so she fetched Adam from outside. Still, the next day, as she watched Ethan and Adam from her family room window, she wondered why she'd beaten herself up so badly. So what if they'd kissed? It didn't mean she was an evil person. It meant she was human.

She smiled at the way her son mimicked Ethan's hand movements. It pleased her to see how well Thor was doing at picking up nonverbal commands. The dog had really come out of his shell since Ethan had started to work with him. With any luck she could still adopt the dog out to a willing family.

"Mom. Mom. Ethan says we're going for a ride."

She'd been so deep in her thoughts she hadn't even seen her son break away from Ethan and head for the house. She spun in her seat.

"Were you watching us?" he asked, coming to a stop near the open front door.

"Close the door." She shook her head, wondering when he'd ever learn. "And, yes. Of course I was watching. I don't want you to overexert yourself."

"Mo-om."

She shook her head. "What's this about riding?"

Her son's face filled with excitement, and she had to admit, he looked better. He hadn't been outside very long, but just those few short moments in the sun had done him wonders.

"Ethan said Uncle Colt said we could go riding this weekend. I guess Ethan hasn't ridden in years. Did you know his dad is a cowboy? His parents live in Montana or someplace. They live on a big ranch. No power. No electricity. Just cattle."

No. She hadn't known that about him. She suspected there was a lot she didn't know about the man who'd kissed her so passionately.

Her face heated.

She hoped Adam didn't notice. Her son had the eyes of an eagle, and all she needed was for him to notice her reaction to Ethan. For such a sick little boy, he seemed obsessed with the idea of her dating someone.

"I'm not sure a ride is a good idea."

"Mo-om," he repeated.

"You're just getting over a bad flu bug. I don't think you should exert yourself."

"That's the point, Mom." He stared up at her as if she was an idiot. "The horse does all the work."

Yup. Definitely on the road to recovery. In a lot of ways. He'd been such a little boy when he'd been diagnosed with leukemia. For the first time she saw a glimpse of the young man he would become.

"How about we play it by ear?"

But she should have known she was fighting a losing battle. Her son was persistent, and he remained blissfully unaware of her desire to avoid Ethan. The trouble with that resolve, however, was the shame she felt every time she knew Ethan was outside working or feeding or helping with her dogs. She'd been communicating with him through her brother, and every time she did, her shame only grew. The man had opened up to her, told her of his fears and his anxiety; he'd kissed her after, and she'd kissed him right back. Now all she did was hide in her house and it really was ridiculous.

"Damn it," she muttered. She needed to stop acting like a hermit. As Chance had said, she needed to go out and have fun, not that riding was her idea of fun, but it would be good to get out.

She just wished it wasn't with Ethan.

Chapter Ten

She didn't have horses of her own, Ethan learned. The family kept all the livestock at the main ranch. So he waited like a kid on his first day of school. Impatient. Excited. Anxious.

Not the same type of anxiety as before.

He wasn't quite himself yet, not by a long shot. He still had the dreams—those terrible dreams—but staying at Misfit Farms, throwing himself into the care of their animals, and then during this past week even riding for the first time in ages, had helped. He still had the dreams about Trevor, but he doubted he'd ever get over the tragic loss of his friend. And he still had moments where it was all he could do to hang on, but things were better. Day by day. That was how he lived.

And today he'd get to see Claire.

He knew she'd been avoiding him. That was okay. She would learn that he felt just as bad about their kiss as she likely did. He didn't have a home, a job—well, not a permanent one, anyway—and he still had some serious issues to deal with. He had no business dragging a woman into his mess of a life. No business at all. Especially when that woman had her own problems to deal with.

"Dr. McCall!"

He turned away from the horse he was in the midst of grooming and smiled. If there was one bright spot to his days, it was Adam. The boy had recovered so quickly it seemed almost like a miracle, but as he glanced past him to his mother, he still saw concern in her eyes.

"Well, look at you." He smiled again at the

little boy running down the middle of the barn aisle. "No more zombie-pale skin and bags under your eyes."

The boy's feet sent up a cloud of dust as he came to a halt. He had a grin about as wide as the Mississippi. "I haven't had a fever in days."

He said it as if days were a month and it made Ethan shake his head. Nothing like the resilience of youth. Sometimes he wished he was back on his parents' ranch, back before they'd sold out and gone to work for one of the big operations in Montana.

"You still need to take it easy." He would have ruffled the kid's hair except he wore his usual baseball cap, this one with the initials of a popular comic book series, his hair having really grown since he'd first met him. He had way more than peach fuzz now. "You don't want to relapse."

Adam shook his head. "Doctor said I was

A-okay. Had a test yesterday and he said my blood looked good."

Claire had walked up behind Adam, her long black hair reaching past her midriff. She wouldn't look at him, and so he had the perfect opportunity to study her. Still the most beautiful woman he'd ever seen, and not just because of her thick black hair and green eyes. No. It was more that there was a goodness to her, an edge of sadness that haunted her eyes and made her beauty the kind that seemed almost ethereal. Two hundred years ago the great masters would have clamored to paint such an enigmatic face. It was too bad her character had been formed by sadness.

"Is that true? Did he pass a vet check?"

It was a joke. A veterinary term that applied to animals, not little boys, and something he hoped would make her smile because he didn't want to become just another problem to her. He wanted to help. Wanted her to know that whatever may have happened, they would always be friends.

"He did." She met his gaze, and he spotted something like relief. Relief that he hadn't tried to swoop in and kiss her again? Or relief for her son? "Said so far so good."

Her underlying meaning that her son's health might all change. And it might, but he didn't like the way she focused on the negative. Life was too short for that. He'd learned the lesson all too well.

"So you up for a ride?" he asked Ethan.

"Yup."

"Let me go get your horse, then."

Colt had shown him the pony-sized quarter horse that served as Adam's mount. It was the weekend, which meant Colt and Natalie were on the road, this time with some clients. They were all at a horse show. Natalie had joked that Colt looked like a fish out of water at the equestrian events in his cowboy boots and hat, but that secretly he loved all the attention.

"Do you know where his pony is?" Claire asked.

"Colt showed me." He forced himself to hold her gaze. She returned his the same way. It was as if she faced off with him. As if she dared him to mention their kiss. He wouldn't, though. He would act as if it hadn't happened. That was what he silently told her. She seemed to understand, because she looked away and her whole body seemed to relax. Yup. Definitely relieved.

"He told me you keep your own horse in the last stall on the left and that I'm not supposed to help you because you love saddling and grooming all on your own."

Claire whipped around to face him. Someone snorted. Adam, he realized, the child releasing something that could only be called a guffaw. He glanced back at Claire, who had an expression of disbelief mixed with amusement on her face.

"That's what he told you, huh?" she asked. For the first time she smiled, a big grin, one that caught him off guard. "What an ass."

"Excuse me?"

"She hates horses," Adam said with a hooting laugh. "That's why she does dogs."

"Not true," Claire quickly amended. "I like them just fine. They just don't like me."

He stared at her, stunned. He would have thought she'd be as horse crazy as the rest of her family. Come to think of it, though, there were no horses on her property. Just dogs. And no pictures of horses. No horse tack. No cowboy boots. Nothing to indicate she carried the horse-crazy gene.

"Then why did your brother insist I take you for a ride?"

"Because he knows I won't let Adam go on a trail ride without me."

"She's a control freak," Adam said.

"Hey." She frowned down at her son.

"It's true. Even Uncle Colt says so." The boy shook his head at the ridiculousness of it all, as if he were the adult and his mother the child.

"I'm only allowed to ride in the arena if she's not around. If she's here, I can ride outside the arena, but only down the road and back. I can't go out on trails all by myself." He ticked the rules he had to follow off with his fingers. "Well, I can go if Uncle Colt takes me, but she's a stress mess that whole time and it kind of ruins the fun of things, knowing she's back at the ranch pacing back and forth."

"I do not pace."

"You do, too."

"And you make me sound like a freak."

"You are about horses, Mom."

Ethan watched the play of emotions across her face. It fascinated him. No, *she* fascinated him, because he suspected there was more to the story of why she didn't like horses than she let on.

"I just prefer to keep an eye on you," she said to her son.

"And I don't blame her." He tapped the bill of Adam's baseball cap. "Go get your pony."

The kid shot off. That left them alone for the first time since Adam had been sick, and he could tell it instantly made her uncomfortable.

"Don't worry. I'm not going to jump you."

Her gaze shot to his. "Excuse me?"

"You look like a cat in a bathtub."

She tipped her chin up. "That's because I'm about to do something I don't like."

"It's because I kissed you." He had no idea why he pushed the matter, especially when he'd vowed to put the incident behind him. But push her he did, for some reason enjoying the way her face blazed with color and the way her jaw ticked in… Was it annoyance? Or maybe it was embarrassment. He couldn't tell.

"What horse did Colt say I should ride?"

And now she was trying to change the subject.

"I'm assuming the horse in the last stall on the left, like he said."

She nodded and turned in that direction. He stepped in front of her. She glanced up, green eyes wide, and he told himself to leave the matter alone. To reassure her that he wasn't going to try to kiss her again. Tell her that he knew it'd been a mistake, a moment of weakness, for both of them.

Instead he found himself saying, "Don't forget. You were the one who started it when you touched me out by the creek."

And it was all there in her eyes. Dismay. Shame. Anger. Pride. "That won't happen again." She slipped past him without a backward glance.

"No?" he teased, though for the life of him he didn't know why.

Leave her alone, a voice warned. *You're pushing her.*

She swung back around to face him. "No." She lifted her chin. "It won't."

SHE GRUMBLED UNDER her breath the whole time she saddled up Blue inside the barn, not just because of Ethan's sudden alpha-male attitude, but because she truly didn't want to ride.

You're doing this for Adam.

That's what she needed to focus on. Her son and the happiness that shone from his eyes whenever he was near a horse. Not the ridiculous man who teased her about something she had deemed a mistake and that she tried desperately to put from her mind.

"You ready?"

She turned to face him. And there she went again, and it really drove her nuts, too. Every time she saw him she couldn't help but think, *oh, my.* She'd had the same thought when she spotted him outside the barn, the horse he'd been grooming like the backdrop of a photo shoot, one with the caption, "Real men wear jeans," or something like that. He wore a black cowboy hat, one that hung low on his forehead, the brim of it curved in such a way that it made the line of his jaw seem more square.

"As ready as I'll ever be." She tried to smile, failed and pretended a sudden interest in Blue's bridle.

"Come on." He smiled. "It's time to quit stalling."

What? She wasn't stalling. She would have told him that very thing except he'd already walked back toward the front of the barn. Outside, her son held the reins to his bay horse, his weight shifting from foot to foot, as if he had to go to the bathroom, but she knew Adam was merely anxious to leave.

"Mo-om."

"Sorry." She hadn't even noticed they were done tacking up. If she had, she would have brought her own horse outside instead of dilly-dallying inside.

Stalling.

Well, okay. Yes. Stalling.

She tugged Blue forward, temporarily blinded when she joined them. It was one of those days where the sky seemed enhanced by a photo filter, the kind that made everything more vivid: the blue of the sky, the orange of the wild poppies in the field out behind Colt and Natalie's house. The green of the trees off in the distance. Her own small house had been built against one of the low hills that dotted the landscape, but Colt's was out in the open. Her dad claimed that had been done on purpose. His great-grandfather had wanted to be able to keep an eye on his stock at all times and so he'd plopped down a homestead in the middle of nowhere. The home she lived in had been built for the ranch foreman. It was far smaller than Colt's, but that was okay. She didn't need two stories and a huge attic. She much preferred her cozy cottage.

"You going to get on?"

She realized she'd been standing there, staring at Colt's big white ranch house. She shook her head to clear it, and when that didn't work, took a deep breath and faced the saddle.

Here we go.

It'd been so long, but it was impossible to forget how to mount a horse. Once you mastered the skill it was like riding a bike. Her foot slid easily into the leather stirrup. Her hands instantly found the reins. She pulled herself up and over with an ease that was both familiar and troubling.

Troubling?

Yes, troubling, because it brought back memories, none of them good.

"Let's go." Adam's excited voice could be heard across the plains. He clearly couldn't wait to get out into the open, because he made a beeline to the gate to the right of her brother's house. He had leaned over and worked the metal bar free before she could tell him to wait. She knew what would happen after Adam got through that gate. Sure enough, he pointed his pony toward the hills.

"Adam."

"Be right back."

"You're still not well—"

He galloped off.

"Adam!"

"Let him go."

She turned in her saddle to face him. "He's just getting over a bad flu."

"And he's fine now."

And there, right there, was the problem with ever getting involved with him. He didn't understand. Adam would never be "fine." Not for a lot of years. Though his blood tests showed they were clear of the cancer for now, that was just it. *For now.* There would be monthly monitoring.

Then bimonthly. Then every six months. And at any moment—*boom*—they could be back where they started. She would worry about her son's health until the day she died. She wouldn't wish that kind of worry and fear on her worst enemy, much less someone like Ethan with his own cross to bear.

"He's not as strong as he once was."

"He will be if you let him spread his wings a little."

Good Lord, he sounded like her brother, right down to the no-nonsense tone. "It's not that simple."

"No," he surprised her by saying. "It probably isn't, but if there's one thing Trevor's death has taught me it's that bad shit happens."

She almost laughed because she'd learned the lesson early in life. That was what her whole life had been like. One series of bad things after another, and the thought cracked open the door to a memory of watching Marcus during his final days. Of watching him struggle to hang on. He'd been exposed to something over there, a bad batch of vaccine that had wrecked his immune system in the same way cancer did. They tried everything, but nothing had been able to stop the progression of the disease until just a shell of Marcus remained. She'd held his hand, begging him to stay, a part of her wanting him to let go, too, because there was nothing on this Earth worse than watching a loved one die.

Nothing.

Adam whooped, bringing her back from her thoughts.

"You look upset."

She moved her horse through the gate she hadn't even realized he held open.

"I just don't like riding much."

He rode one of her other brother's horses, Frosty, an old rope horse that didn't get much use while Chance was in the military. "That surprises me, having grown up on a ranch." He patted Frosty's gray neck when the horse grew antsy about being left behind.

"Why?" she asked, forcing the horrible memories away. Marcus was gone. Remembering those final days did nothing but bring her down, so she took a deep breath, pulling her horse to a stop and waiting for him to close the metal gate held up by matching posts. "Just because a farmer grows corn doesn't mean he likes to eat it."

He smiled briefly as Frosty settled down. "Can't argue that."

She hoped he would leave the matter alone. After he closed the gate and joined her, they rode along in silence for a moment and the fresh air did her good. This was the here. This was the now. She needed to look toward her future.

"Adam told me your dad ruined riding horses for you."

She glanced up at him and she had to marvel. Last month he'd been far away, on another continent, and now here he sat atop a horse looking as if he'd been riding Frosty his entire life. One day soon her brother Chance would be doing the same thing.

"My son thinks he knows a lot of things, but he really doesn't." She forced herself to stare between her horse's ears. "He likes to think he's all grown-up, too."

"Maybe he is."

"Excuse me?"

"Not really. I mean, I know he's only six, but you should let him have fun more often."

She wasn't certain how they'd gone from her troubled past to her son again so quickly, but she found herself clutching the reins, Blue instantly reacting by tossing his head.

"At least while he's feeling up to it," he added.

She opened her mouth, prepared to tell him he was wrong. That it was her job to protect her son. But when she glanced ahead it was to note that Adam had stopped. He had turned back to face them, waved, and even as far away as he'd run, she could still see his smile. It blazed like the gleam of quartz.

"See," Ethan said. "Look at that smile."

She waved back halfheartedly. Adam turned away and rode off again. She looked at the worn leather of her saddle horn. At her horse's mane. At the reins in her hand, the smell of them both comforting and familiar, and took a deep breath. "What if one day I have to let him go forever?"

Clearly, her memories of Marcus were closer to the surface than she thought.

"You won't."

"You don't know that."

"And you don't, either."

She shook her head, reminded yet again of the differences between them. He'd been marred by tragedy once, and look what it'd done to him. She'd been marred by tragedy her whole life and he had no idea what it'd done to her. No idea at all.

"How did your dad ruin riding for you?"

She wasn't going to tell him, but something about the look in his eyes, something about his words made her straighten in the saddle. "He used to beat the crap out of me if I didn't do it right."

She'd shocked him. That was good. She needed to keep him at a distance, not to feel twinges of desire whenever she looked into his eyes, because she did, damn it. He did something for her. What, she didn't know, but she didn't like it. She'd already let herself slip once. Not again.

"Seriously?"

She nodded. "My brothers and me. Colt got the worst of it. He ran off to the Army to get away from it all. Chance used the military to get away, too. They both tried to shield me from it, but my dad kept pushing and pushing and so one day I did what he asked. I fell off in front of him. From that day forward I refused to ride. He tried to shame me into getting back on and when that didn't work, he hit me, hard. Colt stepped in and then Chance. They're older and they both protected me and I think my dad knew in that moment that he was outmanned and outnumbered. He never asked me to ride again. It wasn't until Colt came back that I did it again. It wasn't as bad as I thought it would be, but I still don't really like it. Crazy when you think about it, given our family's ties to the rodeo industry."

Too many memories.

"Is that why you're so overprotective? Because of your dad?"

She pulled her horse to a stop. "I am not overprotective."

"I don't mean to offend." He pulled up on Frosty's reins, too, the horse tossing his head. "I just noticed you really keep Adam under your thumb."

"Wouldn't you? The kid has cancer."

"*Had.*"

"What?"

"Colt told me he's in remission, that they think they have the cancer licked."

"They don't know that for sure."

"Nobody knows anything for sure, Claire."

He fixed his eyes on her. It was an unblinking stare. Serious. And she wanted to argue, she really did, but she couldn't think of a single thing to say, because Adam's doctor had said exactly those words last month, and so she looked away. Their big concern was getting his immune system up to par, but even that looked promising. He'd gotten over that flu all on his own, and without a trip to the hospital.

Adam had reached the top of a small hill. He crested it, disappearing down the other side. She was about to call him back when she felt a hand on her thigh. It surprised her so much she turned to face him.

"I think we *both* need to focus on the here and now."

She opened her mouth to comment but he leaned forward and kissed her. Just a soft brush of his lips, because they were on horseback and his horse shifted, and suddenly he had to pull up on the reins, but even that gentle touch had the ability to rob her of breath. When he straightened in the saddle again and she looked into his eyes she knew he felt it, too. There was a connection between them, something almost otherworldly and inexplicable. This man knew her in a way that made no sense, given the short time they'd spent together. It frightened her. It was why she reacted to his touch the way she had the other day. Why, God help her, she didn't want their kiss to end.

"Where did Adam go?" she mumbled to cover her confusion and the fear that suddenly blossomed in her heart.

"Claire."

She kicked Blue into a gallop.

"Claire," he called out again.

But just because she didn't like to ride didn't mean she didn't know how. She was a hell of a rider and she knew it, and so she didn't listen. Blue made it easy with his smooth gaits. So she galloped, faster and faster, running up the small hill, relieved to find Adam on the other side, waiting, green eyes wide.

"Wow, Mom," he said as she pulled to a stop next to him. "You actually *do* know how to ride."

No. She knew how to escape. How to run away from something that scared the crap out of her.

Chapter Eleven

He'd frightened her off.

She hadn't said a word for the rest of the ride, had somehow managed to keep Adam between the two of them as they traveled toward the line of trees and the base of the foothills. He shouldn't have kissed her, damn it, but he hadn't been able to resist the way she'd looked sitting there, black hair coiled over her shoulder in a ponytail, green eyes haunted by the ghosts of her past. She had been through so much, way more than he had, and she'd somehow held on to her sanity. She had him beat in that department.

They headed back after she took him to what

she called the stock pond, but was really a small lake, Adam begging her to go swimming.

"Not today," she told him.

Adam's face fell.

"But we can come back next week."

The kid jerked his head up so quickly Ethan almost laughed. "Seriously?"

"If you want."

"Woo-hoo!"

He rode off, a fist pumping in the air, the other holding the reins. Ethan smiled. He tried to move his horse up next to Claire's to tell her he approved, but she rode off, not that she probably cared for his opinion. Still, he considered it a minor victory. Maybe some of what he'd said earlier had sunk in.

They arrived back at the ranch an hour after they'd left, and he had to admit, Adam looked pretty tuckered out. He helped the boy unsaddle his horse, and by the time he'd finished, Claire was there, observing. She smiled her goodbyes, and Ethan watched her go, wondering why her silence bothered him so much. Their kiss might have been brief, but he'd felt something. She'd felt it, too.

And that's what bothers you.

She refused to acknowledge it.

He didn't see her for the rest of the week, not even when working with Thor. He'd been half-tempted to check in on her, but he gave her space instead. He needed to do some thinking of his own, not just about Claire and where their relationship was headed, but about his own life and how he'd let Trevor's death affect him. Claire had lost so much more than he had over the years: her childhood, her husband, very nearly her son—and yet she still stood strong. Damn, he admired her.

Colt and Natalie kept him busy that week. In addition to moving forward with turning Misfit Farms into a stallion station, he'd held an impromptu vaccination clinic for all the horses in their care. It'd been a huge success, so much so that he'd gotten a call from Natalie's friend, Mariah Johnson, a local vet. She wanted to know if he'd be interested in covering for her while she went out on maternity leave. He hadn't known what to say. He still wanted to train dogs—his work with Thor had emphasized how much he still wanted to do that—but he also liked working at the farm. And right now, the pickings were pretty slim. He'd posted his résumé on a site for veterinarians, but the only places he'd heard back from were big city animal clinics, places he didn't want to go. Being in the country had taught him that much.

His cell phone rang, Ethan so deep in thought he picked it up without even thinking.

"Ethan?" The voice on the other end of the line sounded vaguely familiar, but it took him a moment to bring his thoughts back to Earth, or back to where he sat in his loft above the barn.

"Yes," he answered tentatively.

"It's me," said a soft, Southern drawl.

Recognition dawned, and he sat up in his chair.

"Red?" It had been Trevor's nickname for his wife, and just the sound of it had the ability to kick him in the gut all over again. For the first time in nearly a week his hands started to shake.

"You sound surprised to hear from me."

"Yes. I mean, no, no, of course not. I told you to call me anytime."

"Well, I guess it was time, then."

He heard the smile in her voice, probably forced, because he doubted she could be any more over her husband's death than he was. Despite his words to Claire the other day, it was still hard for him to put one foot in front of the other. The only thing that seemed to help was working with Colt and Natalie's horses. He thanked God for them every day because without them he doubted he would have made it this long without help of the psychological kind. In fact it'd given him an idea, one he wanted to explore at some point in the future when his future was settled.

"How are you?" he asked.

"Hanging in there. You?"

"Same."

He looked out the window of his apartment above the barn, trying to lose himself in the view. It was one of those days, the kind when the sky looked burned to a crisp after being scorched by the sun. Out beyond the big red barn the horses grazed contentedly. Way out where he and Claire had kissed, a lone deer stood, ears flicking, nose sniffing the air.

"It's good to hear your voice," she said softly.

He almost asked how the kids were. Hell, he was godfather to one of them, but he knew they couldn't be good. They'd been as grief-stricken over their father's death as he had. He could only imagine what it was like for Naomi. Of course, she'd coped without Trevor before his death. The onerous life of a military wife. They had to be some of the most resilient women on God's green Earth.

She'd grown quiet and he wondered if she thought about the last time they'd spoken to each other. They'd been at Trevor's grave site. It'd been a cloudy day. More than a few members of their unit had already left but the two of them had still been standing there, wind blowing, rain threatening, both of them staring down at the casket at the bottom of a rectangle-shaped hole.

"You sleeping?" he asked, as inane and stupid a question as he'd ever asked.

No response, not right away at first. "Not very well. It's T.J. He has nightmares."

"Yeah, but he doesn't know—" About the explosion. The way Trevor died. He didn't want to say the words out loud, but she picked up on them nonetheless.

"No. Of course not." She paused as if she shook her head. "He just wants his daddy back."

Ethan's stomach flipped. He couldn't even imagine, but as the silence stretched on once again, he began to sense there was more to her call than he thought.

"Is there something I can do for you?"

She paused and he knew she gathered her thoughts. "Well." She took a deep breath, and he could imagine her standing there in the small kitchen he'd visited once before, back when he and Trevor had been on leave, the children, Samantha and T.J., watching TV in the background, the smell of home-cooked food hovering in the air. "I was wondering if you might know where Janus is?"

And there it was. The question he'd been half expecting. He'd known it might happen, had half hoped it would. It'd been part of the reason why he'd followed Claire to her hometown. He'd wanted to keep tabs on the dog. To be there just in case Red called.

"As a matter of fact I do."

He heard her sigh, knew of her relief based on the way she paused for a moment trying to gather her words the way a child did before asking for a special treat. "I've been thinking about him a lot lately," she finally admitted. "Thinking about what Trevor would want me to do."

He would have wanted the dog to be with his family. Ethan had tried to tell her that after it'd all happened. He'd tried to convince her Janus would be a great family dog. Trev would have been horrified to know his faithful companion would be sent to strangers. That, too, was why he'd gone to Claire. He'd wanted to reassure himself somehow that the dog would be taken care of. He'd also wanted to reassure Janus, because despite what people might think, canines were as smart as their human counterparts. Janus knew. He'd been next to his master when he'd died. Had tried to crawl over to him even as injured as he'd been. Had licked his hand. The dog knew. He would stake his life on it.

"I think I should take him." He heard her take a deep breath. "I mean, I don't know how I'm going to manage it. Two kids, no husband and a military dog, but it's what he would want."

Ethan felt such relief in that moment that his knuckles hurt from clutching the cell phone so hard. "Do you have a pen?"

"Yeah."

"I'm going to give you directions."

"To where?"

"To Canine Pet Rescue, where Janus is."

"You have the address of the rescue memorized?"

"Of course I do." He smiled. "I live there."

SHE WAS *NOT* a coward.

Claire just felt like one as she rushed around

the house like a crazy woman before Ethan came over.

With a woman.

She hadn't heard from him all week and then suddenly he'd called and told her he was bringing someone over. Someone he wanted her to meet and that she wanted to adopt Janus. A female friend. He hadn't even given her time to explain that things didn't work that way. He couldn't just handpick someone to adopt one of her dogs. She had a waiting list. Besides, Janus wasn't ready to be adopted. He still hadn't recovered from his wounds.

You just don't like that he's bringing over a woman.

That didn't matter, she firmly told herself. She just didn't like his high-handedness. It didn't help that her brother and Natalie sang his praises up to heaven and back. He was a huge help, they said. They were trying to convince him to stick around. Natalie claimed half of her clients were in love with him. She'd wanted to bury her head in her hands when she and Adam had gone over for dinner a few days ago.

"They're here."

Adam came tearing out of his back room. She almost told him to slow down, but she didn't.

Let him have more fun.

And she couldn't argue the point because Ethan was right. Adam needed to laugh and smile and be more like other boys. She did keep too close a watch on him. It'd weighed on her to the point that she'd agreed to let Adam ride one of Colt's trick horses, something her son had been dying to do, and not just around the ranch, but at an upcoming rodeo. They would all be attending the rodeo and Adam would be a star attraction. Adam had been in hog heaven all week. He'd probably be at his uncle's ranch right now except he clearly wanted to meet Ethan's friend. He blew by Claire so fast he just about knocked her off her feet. He opened the door just as fast. A gorgeous redhead stood outside.

Wow.

No wonder he wanted to pull some strings. He probably wanted to pull more than that.

She tried to smack the little green monster that reared its ugly head out of her mind, but that she couldn't do. In her light pink shirt and tight jeans the woman was the picture of elegance and chic. Standing next to Ethan in his black T-shirt and jeans, she looked like his perfect match. He wore no cowboy hat today. The wounds on his arms had healed and the T-shirt exposed them. He was the picture of health and fitness, and so was the woman. Claire felt like a homeless person by comparison in her old black capris and long white T-shirt.

"Where have you been?" Adam asked.

She almost groaned. He'd asked about his new friend insistently. Her son had no idea that Ethan walked over at the crack of dawn every morning. She watched him from behind the lace curtains of her bedroom even though she told herself to close the drapes. She just couldn't seem to stop, and it'd taken her until yesterday to admit the bitter truth. He fascinated her. She watched him work with Thor and sometimes Janus, and she knew he had to be a good man. Kind. Thoughtful. Soft with his hands. That much she knew from experience, and it made her cheeks turn so red she hoped like hell Ethan and his "friend" didn't notice.

"What do you mean, where have I been?" He walked inside when Adam stepped aside. His friend followed behind, glancing around the house curiously. "I'm here every morning."

Not much to see, she silently told her.

Their gazes met and Claire expected to see disapproval at the meagerness of her surroundings. Instead she saw kindness and a small, friendly smile, one that lit the woman's blue eyes.

"In the morning," her son repeated. "My mom

said you come by during the day, when we're out, because you don't want to bother us."

She did not say that. Well, maybe she'd implied it, but her son's words made her face flame even more. "I just meant you're busy," she quickly amended.

Did he know she watched him in the mornings? Did he feel her stare? Wasn't it weird and slightly stalker-like that she even did that?

She refused to answer her own question. Instead she took a deep breath and prepared herself for looking into his jade-green eyes. When she finally did everything froze inside her because she saw amusement there.

He *did* know.

She wanted the Earth to open up and swallow her whole.

"Naomi, this is Claire, the woman I was telling you about."

Okay, get it together.

She transferred her gaze to the woman, whose

friendly smile widened. She came forward, and the hand she held was as slender and fine as a bird's wing.

"So nice to meet you, Claire."

Her name had come out sounding like *Clai-air*. So Southern it made her crave pralines and cream, even though she'd never had them before.

"Nice to meet you."

The hand that shook her own slipped from her gasp. She saw the woman's smile falter a bit, saw something else, too, something both familiar and heartbreaking.

Sadness.

It clung to the woman like an old dress.

It hit her then who she was. Trevor's widow. Janus's old handler. No wonder…

"Mrs.—" Goodness. She'd completely forgotten his best friend's last name. "Ma'am," she quickly amended. "I'm so sorry about your loss."

The woman's eyes sparked in a way that silently tried to reassure her. "Thank you."

"You were married to Trevor?"

They both turned to Adam, who still stood near the door, watching the scene with curiosity in his eyes.

"I was." Naomi smiled at her son. "And you must be Adam."

Her son nodded. "Dr. Ethan told me you have kids."

"I do." She glanced back at Claire. "They're with their grandparents this weekend. I was hoping I can keep what we're doing here a secret. I don't want them disappointed if it doesn't work out."

So she wasn't expecting to just take the dog. The words had the ability to drain the tension from Claire's shoulders. "You want to go see him?"

The woman took a deep breath and Claire realized how hard this would be for her. She'd never had a handler's widow show up for a dog. It was a first for her and something she knew wouldn't be easy.

Adam had lurched forward. He opened the door. Claire watched as Ethan went to Naomi and lightly touched her arm, the silent gesture of support making her look away for a moment. Did he have a thing for his best friend's widow? But the moment she thought it she dismissed it. Ethan wasn't the type to do something like that. He had clearly loved his friend, and that love extended to his friend's widow, nothing more.

It was chilly outside for a midsummer day. The fog had reached its silky fingers inland, hovering over the hills all day and hanging high overhead. A sheen of moisture clung to the roses along the front of her house even though it was late afternoon, the smell of dank earth and wet leaves filling the air. It was a comforting smell. The smell of her childhood back before her mother had died and everything had gone to hell.

"Nice place," Naomi said.

No. Not really. Some of her sister-in-law's clients had nice homes. Big homes. Her home was small and out in the middle of nowhere but it was all her own. She didn't have a mortgage and she didn't have to worry about neighbors complaining about her dogs, and in the years since she'd taken it over she had made it her own. She'd been the one to plant the roses. Had laid down a cobblestone pathway to the door. She'd even added a sprinkler system that watered twin patches of grass on either side of the stones. Between a widow's pension and her work as a freelance graphic artist, it all came together. The dogs, CPR, that was all a labor of love. A time-consuming labor, but as she watched Trevor's widow walk toward Janus, it reminded her that it was all worth it. She knew immediately which dog had been her husband's because her eyes had settled upon Janus sitting in the middle of his dog run, ears pricked forward. The other dogs paced. Some barked. A few peeked out from their kennels. Well, all but Thor. Janus simply sat there and stared, and Claire knew that Naomi had met the dog many times before.

"Did you want me to bring him out?" she asked.

"Sure."

They all stopped near the corner of the dog runs. Claire headed for the tool shed to grab a leash.

"I'll help," Adam said. Her son ran ahead to open the chain-link door.

"Adam, no—"

Janus didn't hesitate. He burst past her son so fast he nearly knocked him down. He nearly knocked Claire off her feet, too.

"Janus, *hier*," Claire called.

But the dog was on a mission. Claire watched

as he made a beeline for Naomi, rearing back when he was a couple feet away, Claire crying out, "No," right as Janus thrust two big paws through the air.

Naomi didn't miss a beat. She opened her arms, welcoming the dog paws on her pretty pink shirt, sinking to the ground at the same time she buried her head in the dog's black fur.

"Janus," she heard Naomi say, but in a voice thick with tears. The dog wiggled free, licking tears off Naomi's face, his tail wagging so hard, it rocked his whole back end and Claire started to smile. Naomi scrubbed her fingers through the dog's fur and Claire realized she still wore her wedding ring, the sight making her throat tighten. Janus had become so excited he made little yelping noises.

"Wow," Adam said.

Claire wiped tears from her face. Yeah, wow. No question that the dog recognized the woman, and that she held a special place in the canine's heart. The mate of his former master, and he loved her the way his master had no doubt loved her.

"I guess Janus has a new home."

"No," Adam said. "Janus is going home."

Chapter Twelve

A match made in heaven, Ethan thought, watching as Naomi signed her name with a flourish.

"And that's all there is to it," Claire said with a huge smile, one that made it seem she might be on the edge of tears.

"Congratulations," Ethan offered with a grin of his own.

It was a smile Naomi returned, the first smile he'd seen on her face since he'd returned to the States. "The kids are going to be so excited."

"I'm sure they are," Claire agreed. "You can bring them out here when you pick up Janus."

"Are you kidding? I'm going to surprise them."

She probably didn't mean to, but Claire finally glanced in his direction, her smile slipping a notch, and Ethan wondered if he'd pushed her too far the other day. He should have never gotten on her case about her son. He didn't regret kissing her, though. That had been the highlight of his week.

"Did you want to stay for dinner?" Claire asked with what Ethan knew was a polite smile.

"No, no." Naomi shook her head so that her red hair fell behind her shoulders. "I'll be back tomorrow with a proper kennel for Janus." Her eyes slid away from Claire and settled on him. "Walk me out?"

"Sure." He smiled at Claire, observing the way she couldn't quite look him in the eyes. "I'll be right back."

"Wait. Is she leaving?" Adam came rushing out of the family room, where he'd been playing a video game. He didn't have his ball cap on and Ethan noticed his hair had really started to come back in. He looked like a regular kid.

"I am," Naomi answered.

The little boy didn't wait for permission before racing up to his new friend and giving her a hug. Naomi looked up at them awkwardly before patting the boy on his head.

"Thank you for taking Janus," Adam mumbled into her shirt. "He's going to be so much happier back with his family."

Naomi looked close to tears all of a sudden. She leaned down and hugged Adam back. "I think he will be, too."

When she straightened he could tell she was touched by Adam's words. Her smile was warm when she glanced in Claire's direction. "Thanks for taking such great care of my husband's dog."

"You're welcome."

"I'll be back tomorrow."

Ethan held the door as Naomi slipped past.

They both stepped out into the dank, evening air. It seemed like hours since they'd gone out to the kennel to see Janus, but it'd been less than two. The sun had begun to sink behind the mountains, and because it was overcast, it was darker than he expected. Clouds still hung overhead, but it wasn't so dark that he couldn't see his friend's face.

"I'll arrange for someone to check his wounds for you."

"That would be great."

"Although he's healing nicely."

She nodded. "He's had excellent care."

"Yes, he has."

Naomi peeked up at him. "She's a nice lady."

Ethan nodded. "Yes, she is."

"With a lot on her plate."

"Yup. Just like someone else I know."

She paused near the edge of the yard, if one wanted to call the tiny patch outside Claire's house a yard. There were no boundaries, just a patch of grass that faded into burned pasture.

"She's strong," Naomi said. "Stronger than me."

"I think you're both pretty remarkable."

"Nah. At least my two kids are healthy."

His smile fell. "Yeah. She's been through a lot."

Naomi glanced back at the house, sadness in her eyes. "I look at her, and what she's been through, and I think, stop feeling sorry for yourself."

"She makes me feel the same way."

"She brings it all into perspective. I miss Trevor so much, but I didn't go through the horrors of watching my kid suffer through chemo and radiation and God knows what else all the while trying to hold my life together. And before that, what she went through with her husband. Claire Reynolds deserves a medal."

She was right, and it made him think that

maybe that was why his anxiety had improved even if the bad dreams hadn't. What did he have to be afraid of compared to what she'd been through? That day when she'd climbed aboard the horse despite the bad memories they evoked. Selfless. That's what it'd been. She lived each day for her son, and for the dogs she rescued, and in honor of the man she'd been married to. He wouldn't be much of a man if he couldn't do the same.

"I don't know that she thinks of herself as heroic," Ethan said. "I think she's just taking it day by day."

"Aren't we all?"

He looked into Naomi's blue eyes, searching her face, for what he didn't know. Approval, maybe.

Approval for what? he wondered.

That he'd done okay. That he hadn't let Trevor down. That she wasn't angry with him or disappointed or that she didn't blame him in some way for her husband's death.

"Ethan?"

He hadn't even realized he stared at the ground or that he'd stuffed his hands in his pockets. His hands had started to shake again, but for a different reason this time. He felt the guilt so much more acutely now that he stood in front of her. When she'd gotten out of the car earlier and he'd seen her for the first time since…

"You okay?"

He sucked in a deep breath of air, forced himself to stand tall and proud as he asked, "Do you blame me?" He pulled his hands from his pocket, though his fingers flexed over and over again into a fist. "For what happened to Trevor?"

Her whole face registered surprise, from the parting of her lips to the widening of her blue eyes. She reached out and grabbed his forearm.

"Oh, my Lord, Ethan, no." She gave his arm a squeeze. "You had no control over that."

He knew that. Deep down inside. He just couldn't seem to stop himself from thinking that way. At night his mind went over it again and again. What if he hadn't delayed those few minutes to check on his canine patients? What if he'd insisted Trevor wait for him? What if he'd been the first one to leave?

"You haven't been blaming yourself, have you?" she asked, her hand tightening even more.

He shrugged. Her hand fell away, but he didn't escape her gaze. "No." Yes. Deep down inside he supposed he did. "Maybe."

She drew up straight. "Would it surprise you to learn that I do, too?"

He saw how seriously she meant the words by the way her gaze held his own. She even nodded before glancing down at the ground.

"Every night as I lie in bed trying to sleep I

wonder if he'd still be alive if I hadn't pressured him to get out." A strand of her hair had fallen next to her cheek. He watched as she tucked it back behind her ear. "Did he tell you about our big fight?"

He shook his head. All he'd ever heard from Trevor was what a saint his wife was. How much she meant to him. How much he loved her.

"We got in a big argument the last time he deployed. I said some things. He said some things. We got over it, of course. I made peace with his decision. Told myself that whatever he decided to do when this last tour was up, I'd be okay with it. And then he called me and told me he was coming home and I realized he did remember our argument and I was so excited—"

She shook her head and closed her eyes, and Ethan knew she was on the verge of tears. He moved toward her, pulling her into his arms. "Shh. It's okay."

She wiggled out of his grasp. "No. It's not okay. It's taken me the past few weeks to admit that it wasn't my fault at all. It was the rotten bastards that attacked your base. But the fact is he had a dangerous job, and I knew that, I should never have added to his stress…"

"No."

"Then you need to stop feeling guilty, too. I know I have." She wiped at her eyes with the heel of her hand. "You still have the dreams?"

He'd told her about them at Trevor's funeral. "A little." She tipped her head sideways. "Okay, a lot."

She wiped at her other eye. "What a pair we are." She turned and stared at Janus. The dog peered over at them, unblinkingly, watching her. It was uncanny. He hadn't seen Trevor's wife in months and yet he remembered.

"And that woman in there would be good for you." She pointed to the house. "I can tell."

He didn't comment. What was the point? She'd clearly read his feelings for Claire on his face.

"You're going to need to push her, though."

"You think?"

"She's going to be a tough nut to crack."

That was an understatement.

"Sick kid. Dead husband. Sucky past. It's a wonder she hasn't sworn off the human race entirely."

"I've been thinking lately maybe I should just give her some space. Get my own head screwed on straight before I ask her out on a date or something. Hell. I'm not exactly ready for a relationship, either."

"Yes, you are." She glanced at the house again, smiled. "Trevor and I used to talk about it all the time. I wanted to introduce you to some of my friends. He told me no. He said you wouldn't be ready to settle down until you left the Army."

"Settle down?" *Whoa, whoa, whoa.* "I like her, but I wouldn't go that far."

"Keep telling yourself that, solider."

He drew back. No. She had it all wrong. He understood Claire. Hell, he didn't deny he was attracted to her. He definitely wanted to date her. When he was ready. When they were *both* ready.

"Naomi, I don't even know which way is up right now. The last thing I need is a woman in my life."

"Trevor would tell you not to let a little thing like that stop you."

Trevor would have loved Claire.

"You're ex-Army. A combat veteran. If you want her, go after her. That's what Trevor would tell you."

"Hoo rah," he muttered under his breath, thinking about the woman inside the house and what she might mean to him.

"Hoo rah," she echoed with a small smile. "So go get her, soldier."

THEY WERE OUT there a long time.

Claire resisted the urge to go to the window and look outside. Whatever they were talking about, it must have been serious, because when Ethan finally came back in, he seemed distracted.

"I'm headed back to my place." He smiled, but it was a weak one.

She used her front door to hold him at bay, the taillights of his friend's car fading down the road.

"You going to walk in the dark?"

"It's not all the way dark yet," he said, his gaze moving past her as if searching for Adam. "Besides, I could really use fresh air right now."

She nodded, suddenly as awkward as a duck in a swimming pool. "Then I guess I'll see you later."

"Tomorrow," he quickly amended, half turning and watching Naomi disappear down the road, too.

"Tomorrow?" she echoed stupidly.

He turned back to face her. "When Naomi picks up Janus and then later, at the rodeo."

The rodeo. Heavens to Betsy, she'd completely forgotten about that. Tomorrow night the annual Via Del Caballo Rodeo started. It was Think Pink night, too. Adam would be doing his own version of a rodeo act—riding her sister-in-law's horse without a bridle in front of the audience— while being honored as a cancer survivor even though she'd argued with Colt that he wasn't officially in remission yet.

Don't think like that, she told herself. Ethan was right. She'd turned into a negative Nellie and she needed to stop.

"Are you going to the rodeo tomorrow, then?"

He nodded. "It'll be the first time I've seen your brother perform in front of an audience and I'm looking forward to it."

"You're in for a treat."

"I've watched him practice, and if it's anything like that, it'll be spectacular. A bunch of Natalie's clients from the barn are going, too. They tell me I have to dress up in pink. Don't know that I have the clothes to do that."

"All you'll need is a shirt. No pink jeans."

He smiled. She froze again. Goodness, what was with her?

If she felt this awkward now, what would it be like tomorrow morning, or worse, tomorrow night when she'd be forced to socialize with him? She clutched the handle of her front door. Just the thought of sitting next to him made her whole insides twist like a rope.

"Well, have a nice walk."

Instead of retreating he took a step toward her. "Do you ever think about life after all this? After Adam is all better and you can move on."

The door handle slipped from her grasp. The

door started to swing closed but he stopped it with his foot.

"No," she answered with what sounded like a croak. "Not really."

"About what you'll do with all your free time?"

She swallowed. Hard. "I can barely think past the next fifteen minutes, much less months from now. Right now, it's one day at a time. Sometimes one minute at a time. Sometimes even one second at a time."

"You should," he said. And with those cryptic words he turned around and walked away. She stood there, the door still open, wondering what the hell that had all been about, and why she suddenly wanted to run.

Straight into his arms.

No. She had to focus on Adam. Tomorrow night Adam would be around a bunch of people, which meant extra precautions and then later on worrying about him coming down with the flu or a cold or something much worse. She didn't have time to think about her future.

And especially not one that might involve Ethan.

Chapter Thirteen

He'd never been to a rodeo before. In all his years working with animals and all the years growing up on a ranch, he'd never been to one, much to his parents' chagrin. As he stood next to Claire in a dirt lot packed with horse trailers and trucks, the sun shining down on their backs, he wondered why. It smelled like animals and popcorn, two scents that shouldn't mix, but strangely did.

"Can you believe I get to ride in grand entry this year?"

"I know." Ethan smiled down at Adam, who stood between him and his mom. They were watching Colt groom a good-looking dark bay horse named Playboy. "That's great."

Claire didn't seem so enthusiastic, or so Ethan thought. Then again, she'd been doing a good job of pretty much ignoring him the whole time he'd been at the rodeo grounds. He wondered if she was upset about Janus leaving this morning, but that didn't make sense. She'd been genuinely happy to help Naomi load up the dog, or so it'd seemed. After Naomi had left, however, she'd made it clear she was too busy to talk to him. She'd disappeared inside the house so fast you'd have thought a tornado was coming. He just didn't understand.

Her brother must have noticed the pinched look on his sister's face because he said, "Relax. He'll be fine."

"He better be." She nervously fidgeted with a strand of her black hair. "If anything happens, I'll kill you."

Of course, she had a right to be a little more

tense than normal. Adam wouldn't be riding in grand entry like a normal kid. No. He'd be riding without a bridle as part of the opening act. They were spotlighting his recovery from cancer. He'd practiced back at the ranch, and that had gone terrifically, but Claire had gotten sick every time she'd had to watch—or so Colt had claimed.

Her brother paused in the midst of brushing the horse's back. "Nothing will happen." He went back to brushing, puffs of dust temporarily filling the air. "You've seen Playboy perform without a bridle a million times. You know how safe it is."

"He's never carried my son before."

Natalie came around the edge of the trailer then, and ironically, she carried Playboy's bridle, her blue eyes settling on Claire. "He has when we practiced at home." She smiled at her sister-in-law. "Believe me, he'll be fine."

Ethan had been told the horse Adam rode was

a champion reining horse that she'd bought to help her overcome a serious riding injury. He knew Colt and Natalie trusted the horse implicitly and so there was no reason to fear. He almost told Claire to relax, too, but he had a feeling that would earn him a glare. He didn't want to be on her bad side. He had plans for Claire later that night, not that she knew anything about it. He caught Colt's gaze right then, the two of them exchanging glances. When he'd told Claire's brother he wanted to take his sister out on a date, Colt had simply said four words: *Leave it to me.*

Operation Claire on a Date had been born.

"How much longer?" Claire asked, shifting from foot to foot. Ethan worried she'd pull that strand of hair out of her head.

"Show starts at one," Colt said. He tugged his cell phone out of his back pocket. "That's in a half hour."

"I'm just not sure standing out in this sun is a good idea."

Sun? What sun?

"Mom. I'm fine."

Ethan had parked behind the rodeo grounds, next to where Colt had parked his giant rig, beneath the shade of a giant oak tree.

"That's what you say now, but then I'll get you home and you'll be burnt to a crisp."

Adam might be a young kid, but he could look like an adult at times and his glare clearly told his mom to take a hike. Ethan almost laughed.

"You ready there, partner?" said another woman, Colt's lead trick rider, a woman who'd recently taken the place of a longtime family friend as head of the Galloping Girlz. Carolina was her name. She had blond hair and eyes the color of a new swimming pool and Ethan sensed she had troubles of her own to bear.

"You bet I am." Adam already wore his pink

shirt, Ethan noticed, as did he. So did everybody, although the trick riders were in pink spandex outfits. Claire, too, had dressed for the occasion, and the color suited her ivory complexion and black hair. She was beautiful standing there watching her son. It amazed him, though, to see how both the crowd and the competitors supported cancer awareness. Even the hardened bull riders wore the color. Plus, Claire had been wrong. They did make pink jeans and the current Miss Via Del Caballo rodeo queen wore them—that and pink chaps.

"All righty, then," Colt said. "We're going to let you warm up a little in the practice pen. Ride around just like you did at home. When we're ready to go into the main arena, I'll drop his bridle."

Adam crammed his straw cowboy hat down on his head as if he were about to get on a saddle bronc. "This is going to be so cool."

He heard Claire release something that

sounded like a hiss and he couldn't help himself. He placed a hand on her shoulder, but it was as if he'd shot her with a cattle prod. She ducked away so fast his hand was left hanging in the air.

"You scared me," she said, turning to face him, hand on her chest.

Had he? Somehow he doubted it. That had been the move of a woman who didn't want to be touched. Who'd put up a barrier between them. No Trespassing. Plus, her complexion was fair enough that he spotted the blush spreading across her cheeks like spilled paint.

"Sorry."

She had refocused her gaze on her son, but she nodded her acknowledgment of his apology. Maybe he should tell her brother to call the whole thing off. What stopped him, however, was the absolute certainty that she needed to get out for a little bit. He might only be taking her to dinner, but it would do her good to let her hair down and socialize with someone other than her own son. Clearly Adam felt the same way. The boy shot him a look that practically begged him to do something about his mother. Ethan almost smiled again.

"All right, let's head on over," Carolina said. "Gonna be center stage today, huh, Adam?" The woman tapped the top of Adam's cowboy hat.

"If my mom doesn't freak out and die of a heart attack first," they all heard him mutter.

Okay, that blew the lid off the smile he'd been holding back. He even chuckled a little before saying, "If she does, I'll take care of her."

Claire glanced over at him, then immediately looked away, and that did it. First this morning and now this. He crossed to her side, brushed her arm with his hand. At least she didn't jerk away this time. Still he saw her tense.

"He'll be fine."

She crossed her arms in front of herself and said, "I know."

"Colt would never let something happen to him."

"I know," she repeated.

"Climb aboard," Natalie said.

"Time to go practice," Colt added, motioning Adam over to Playboy's side. "And remember, when you're out there, listen to Carolina. She's in charge now."

They helped Adam mount up, the smile on the kid's face big enough to spot from space. He all but bounced in the saddle as they moved as a group toward the practice arena out behind where everyone had parked.

A grizzled old cowboy nodded as they walked by. "Colt."

"Hey, Hank."

Ethan had learned Colt was something of a celebrity in the cowboy world, but if he hadn't already known, he would have figured it out by the time they made it to the practice arena. The whole way there he'd been greeted by males and females alike. Ethan knew Colt traveled all over the US performing. His horse was trained to rear and dance and take a bow, all without Colt touching him. Natalie had explained he was booked years in advance, and although he'd cut his performance schedule back since he'd married her, Adam had told him he always made time to perform in front of his hometown crowd.

"You look like you're ready to puke."

They stood by the rail of the warm-up arena; Colt and Natalie stood a little ways away, Claire leaning against the rail as though she needed it for support.

"I'm just tired."

That sounded like a canned excuse, but he didn't push the matter. She'd slipped on thick sunglasses once they'd left the shade of the tree. It was impossible to see her eyes and he found himself wishing he could. She'd been so distant today. More so than ever before. He'd been hoping his question last night might shake her up a bit, but he was beginning to think it'd upset her more than anything else.

"Adam is a heck of a rider." He watched as the kid loped the horse around the pen. The rest of the Galloping Girlz all egged him on. The boy had ridden more this week than he had in a long while and it showed. His pale skin had been bronzed by the sun. His eyes were brighter, too. He looked like a normal, healthy kid in his pink shirt, jeans and cowboy boots. More important, he'd been smiling nonstop since he'd climbed aboard Playboy.

"It's in his genes."

He hadn't expected her to answer, had half thought she'd continue with the silent treatment, and so when she spoke, he found himself thinking maybe things were all right between them after all.

"He told me he wants to be a rodeo rider when he grows up," Ethan said.

"He's been saying that since he was old enough to talk."

"But you refuse to think that far ahead."

Now, why'd he go and push her button? He should be trying to keep the peace, especially in light of the plans he had for later. But he couldn't seem to stop himself.

She went back to watching her son. "I told you last night. One day at a time."

Yes, she had. He'd thought about those words all evening. It was part of why he'd been so determined to take her out this morning. He wanted to fill at least one day with happiness and laughter. She deserved that.

"I guess that's all we can do."

He kept quiet for the rest of Adam's practice session. All too soon they were headed toward the main arena, Ethan following at a distance. Carolina would be carrying the American flag while she stood atop her horse, but the rest of the girls would perform with Colt later on. Still, they all walked over together.

They were nestled against the base of some small hills. The rodeo committee had built grandstands into the slope of the hillside to give spectators a better view of the arena below. Cattle trucks were parked outside, as were horse trailers of every shape and size, some old, some new, some state-of-the art like Colt's. A whole mass of people milled around outside the arena, most of them on horseback, a few trying to make their way through the crowd on foot. Even with as much experience as he'd had around animals it seemed insane to push their way through the hind ends of so many animals, but push through they did until they were at the gate.

"There you are," said a woman with a clipboard when she saw Colt. "We're just about ready to start."

"That's what I figured," Colt said, turning to his nephew. "You know the drill, right?"

"Yup."

"Just the same, I'm going to go over it again. Once the gals carrying the sponsor flags line up in the middle, Carolina here is going to present the American flag while someone sings the national anthem. Once that's finished you'll go in. Just one lap around. That's all. When you're done, you need to go right to the center and stand next to Carolina."

"Yes, sir."

"Then you can lead the crowd out."

"Here comes my flags," said the lady with the clipboard, staring at a group on horseback, each one carrying the flag of a rodeo sponsor. "You'll need to move out of the way."

Ethan almost asked Claire if she wanted to go up to the grandstands, but it was clear she didn't want to move. She had eyes only for her son as they all stepped aside to make way for the horseback riders.

"All right, all right, all right," the announcer said in a Matthew McConaughey voice. "Are you all ready for a rodeo?"

The crowd cheered, the gate swung open and the sponsorship flag team entered at a full run.

"Ladies and gentlemen, welcome to the 51st Annual Via Del Caballo Rodeo."

The audience cheered again, the announcer pausing for a moment to ask the audience to stand as they saluted Old Glory. A young girl walked to the middle of the arena, microphone in hand.

"Have fun," Carolina said, and stood on top of her horse, something that never ceased to fill Ethan with awe, and then entered the arena as the girl started to sing. It was a beautiful performance. Carolina loped along, but her speed built in intensity as the song progressed until as the last glorious verse was sung, she ran at a breakneck speed, blond hair streaming, flag crackling in the wind, arena dust churning.

"Beautiful," Ethan said to Claire, putting his hat back on his head after it was all over. She barely nodded.

"Before we get started with our grand entry, we wanted to remind everyone that today we're dedicating this rodeo to those who're fighting the biggest battle of their life." Ethan looked down at Claire. There wasn't a lick of emotion on her face. "Folks, we know cancer affects one out of two people, and we know most of you know someone who's lost a family member to this horrible disease, so today we thought we'd do something different. Today we thought we'd celebrate the life of a six-year-old boy who's not only surviving, but so far beating cancer."

"You ready?" Colt said.

Adam merely nodded.

Colt moved to the front of Playboy and dropped the bridle. The horse lifted its head, clearly aware that he was about to perform because it seemed he waited for the gate to open. The moment it did, Adam surprised them all by hollering, "Yee ha!" and pounding his heels against Playboy's sides.

"Adam," Claire screamed.

Her son was gone. Playboy pinned his ears and ran as if a legion of hellhounds was at his heels.

"Damn that kid," Colt said.

"He's going to kill himself." Claire sounded ready to faint.

"He'll be okay," Ethan said, placing a hand on her shoulder, because Adam didn't look in danger at all. Playboy kept to the rail, Adam like a flea on his back, the horse's mane and tail streaming.

"Ladies and gentlemen," the announcer said. "Meet Adam O'Brian, nephew to rodeo legend Colt Reynolds and a little boy who's a cancer survivor."

The crowd went wild. Claire covered her mouth with her hand. Adam waved. And when the audience realized Adam rode without a bridle, another round of cries and yells filled the air. Adam just smiled and ran. Just as they'd practiced, Playboy rounded the last corner and headed to the middle. He came to a sliding stop in front of the girls carrying the flags. And there was such a look of pride on Adam's face, such a look of happiness, Ethan felt his throat thicken. He glanced down at Claire. She stared at her son, her hands slowly dropping away, eyes only for the little boy that stood center stage.

"That was perfect," Natalie said.

"Little bugger's going to get an earful when he gets out of there," Colt said. "That was *not* how we practiced it."

"No." Claire half turned. "Natalie's right. That was perfect."

She faced her son again, smiled, turned back

to clap, and it was in that exact moment, outside the Via Del Caballo rodeo arena, that Ethan realized he was falling in love.

Chapter Fourteen

Ethan had been right. One look at Adam's face and Claire knew riding Playboy had been better medicine than a million rounds of injections. As he stood waving and smiling to the crowd, she caught her first glimpse of Adam again. The old Adam. Her son before cancer had taken over their lives.

She had to inhale back her tears. Wouldn't do for her son to see her crying.

A hand had settled on her shoulder. She wanted to shrug it off. Every time Ethan touched her she was reminded of their time in her house, the time she'd lost control.

"He did great."

She nodded and gently eased away from his touch. He didn't try to touch her again, but that was okay. That was how it should be.

She barely heard the rodeo announcers invite everyone into the arena after they introduced Adam. A part of her watched the rodeo queens ride by one by one, their horses galloping hell-bent for leather, their smiles and waves as bright as their crowns. It was as if the Earth had been flipped on its side and everything knocked askew.

"Good job, buddy!" Colt called when it was all said and done.

Adam got to lead everyone out of the arena, a look of pride on his face. He had eyes only for her, she noticed, tears filling her eyes again. Thank God for the sunglasses.

"How'd I do?" he asked her.

"You did great," she said as Colt slipped the bridle back on Playboy's head.

"I'm not sure I liked how you jacked your heels into my horse's sides," Natalie gently scolded.

"I know." Adam had the grace to look abashed. "But I knew you'd never let me run like that with my mom around."

No. She wouldn't. She'd have told him it was too dangerous. That he wasn't ready for the exertion. That he might fall. A million different excuses would have been offered, all under the guise of keeping him safe. But Ethan was right. It was time to let go. Time to move on. Her son wanted that, and because he wanted it, she would learn to live with it, too.

"You were amazing," she heard Ethan say.

She inhaled because there was pride in his voice, too. Pride and approval and joy. For her son.

So what if he loves Adam, she told herself. Because there was that in his voice, too. He cared for her son. She saw it in his eyes when she gained the courage to look up at him.

"Thanks, Ethan," her son said, smiling back.

They all headed toward the parking area, Claire making sure she kept her distance from Ethan. She'd seen him glance at her in puzzlement earlier, and again now as she made sure to keep Playboy between the two of them. He probably thought she was mad at him about his question last night, but that wasn't it at all. When he'd touched her earlier, it had jolted her, to the core. It was that way every time he touched her. Time and distance hadn't done anything to make that stop. If anything, it'd made her crave him more.

Stupid physical attraction.

That was all it was, she firmly told herself. The man did it for her and she had no idea why. Well, aside from the fact that he was good-looking. And kind. And smart. And sweet. And good to her son.

Stop it.

"Did you see my slide stop, Mom?"

"I did."

"That was a *blast*."

"That wasn't in the game plan, either," her brother said.

"I know." Adam's smile was full of pride. "But we pulled it off okay."

"You sure did," Natalie said with a glance at her husband. Colt wouldn't perform until later, toward the middle of the rodeo, when he and the Galloping Girlz would do some impressing of their own.

"Can I do it again?" Adam asked Colt.

"Only if your mom says it's okay."

"Mom?" Adam said, peering back at her from atop Playboy.

"Let me think about it."

That seemed to appease her son. He went back to talking to Colt and Natalie and Carolina and the other Galloping Girlz, she and Ethan trailing behind. She tried not to be aware of him as they crossed between cowboys swinging ropes and horses tied to the rail. He fit right in with his pink-and-white-checkered shirt and off-white cowboy hat. More than one cowgirl had eyed him up and down as he walked past. Those ladies would go completely gaga if they knew he was a veterinarian. That he loved dogs. That he was good with kids. That he knew how to kiss...

What is with *you?*

It was *him*, she admitted. Ethan and his kind words and his sweet touch and the way she'd tossed and turned all night thinking about the way he kissed and how good it felt to have him hold her. Just the thought made her tingle and squirm and flush as she fought off the memory of the touch of his hands.

"I think when we're all done here tonight we should go out and celebrate." It was Colt who spoke the words, and something about the tone caught her attention. "Natalie and I were thinking we could take you to dinner and then ice cream, Adam."

"Cool!"

"We're all going, right?" Claire asked warily.

"Actually, Natalie and I would like to spend time with our nephew all on our own, if that's okay with you. We were even thinking of doing a sleepover." His smile was pure cheese. "You know, like we used to do in the old days."

"Yay!" Adam said with fist to the air.

The sly look Colt shot Ethan made Claire think this wasn't just uncle-nephew bonding time. In fact, she would bet this was all planned. He might try to hide his self-satisfaction behind an innocent smile, but she saw right through him.

"I don't know," she hedged.

"Please, Mom?" Adam pulled on Playboy's reins. They all stopped. "It's been so long since I've been able to spend the night at Uncle Colt's."

Shame on you for using my son like this, she told Colt with her eyes, not that he could see them behind her sunglasses, but he knew what she was thinking.

Colt just smiled. "Let him go. He'll be fine."

You'll be fine. That was what he really meant.

"Please," Adam added again.

She didn't want to, she really didn't, but with everyone staring at her… "Okay, fine."

"Terrific," Colt said. "Ethan, you can take my sister to dinner on your way home."

Pfft. As if she hadn't seen that coming.

"I'd be delighted."

And that, too. She should be furious. She'd spent hours last night convincing herself to keep on staying away from Ethan because despite the way he'd helped her with Adam, she still refused to think about him romantically. Yeah, she desired him. No doubt about that, but it was just physical. Mentally she wasn't ready for him or any other man. She was used to being on her own. Life was comfortable that way. She didn't need the stress of a new relationship.

Even though you want him, taunted a little voice.

Physical, she reminded herself. She would let Colt think he'd gotten one over on her. She'd smile at Ethan and act as if she planned to go home with him, but in fact, they were at her hometown rodeo and she could find her own way home. Ethan wouldn't know what happened until it was too late.

It would be better that way.

SHE'D DITCHED HIM.

Ethan could have cheerfully choked her. He'd looked for her for half an hour before receiving her text.

Caught a ride with a friend. See you later.

"I'll see her later, all right," he muttered, turning down the road that led to her house. Enough of this. They needed to hash out their feelings for each other. He needed to tell her what he'd realized earlier in the evening.

I'm falling in love with you.

He didn't know if she was ready to hear the words or not. Hell, he didn't know if he was ready to say them or if any of this was even real. They'd only met a few weeks ago. It seemed crazy to think he could go from fighting in the Middle East to falling in love with a woman in so short a time, yet there it was.

Her truck was still parked out in front. That was a relief. He'd been worried she'd leave on the off chance he might stop by. It surprised him that she hadn't. Then again, maybe this was part of her plan.

See you later.

Had it been an invitation?

When she swung her front door open he knew that it hadn't.

"What are you doing here?"

Okay. So she really *had* ditched him. She really didn't want to see him. Fine. "We need to talk."

He might not be able to buy her dinner, but he could get to the bottom of her cold shoulder. "About what?"

He took off his cowboy hat, holding it in front of him like a shield. "About why you had a hard time saying two words to me all day? And why you just ditched me. Are you mad at me or something?"

"No." She lifted her chin, her black hair falling over her white T-shirt. She'd changed out of pink and she looked super sexy in a sleeveless tank top loose around her waist but low enough that he had a hard time keeping his gaze on her face. She still wore the jeans, but he suddenly found himself wishing he could peel them off.

"Then what was the problem?"

She shrugged. "I was nervous about my son riding."

Bull. He almost said that very thing except he suddenly noticed that she fidgeted with the door handle. She twisted it back and forth and back and forth. It even slipped from her grasp with a loud *snick*. She gave him a faux smile and went back to twisting it again.

It dawned on him then with a certainty that drove him to take a step closer. He knew what bothered her, and it had nothing to do with fear for her son. Her problem was with *him*.

"Adam was in good hands." He took another step closer.

Her voice sounded raspy as she said, "Adam has been sick."

Another step. Her eyes flicked left and then right, as if she sought to escape. "But he's not sick anymore."

"Technically, he is because he's still not officially in remission."

"Shush."

"Excuse me?" But she held her ground. He

saw it then, the spark of excitement in her eyes. She might pretend indifference, but she was far from that.

"We've been over this a million times before."

"I know, so there's nothing left to say."

"I know that," he said, stepping inside her home before she could close the door on him, and tossing his hat onto the coatrack that stood by the door. "And I agree with you. We shouldn't talk."

"What do you mean?"

"We should do something else."

"Ethan—"

"Are you going to deny you have feelings for me?"

She lifted her chin. "How I feel is irrelevant."

"No, it's not."

He clasped her face between his palms. She tried to pull back, but not very hard. Oh, no. Her eyes invited him closer.

"Shh," he said again, and then he kissed her.

She'd gone completely still, but that was okay because it gave him time to caress those silky soft lips with his own, to sip the taste of her: honey and vanilla. That was what she tasted like. He wasn't content to lightly taste her, though. He wanted all of her and so he tipped his head a bit, increased the pressure, all the while still cupping her jaw with his hands.

She collapsed.

That was how it felt. Her body melted into his, and he found himself dropping his hands to her waist, propping her up. Her mouth opened beneath his, and then her tongue touched his own and it nearly killed him. The smell of her. The taste of her. The way she brushed up against him. The tips of her breasts pressed against his chest and he wanted to bend down and taste each one of them, but he didn't.

He broke off the kiss, tipped his head back. "Lord," he heard himself say. "You're going to kill me."

She breathed hard, too. He could feel those breasts touch him and then retreat, touch him and then retreat, the sensation both erotic and frustrating. As if sensing the direction of his thoughts she shifted in his arms. He thought she might move away, gave her every opportunity to do so, but she didn't.

"What are you doing to me?" She rested her head against his chest.

"Kissing you," he answered.

Fantasizing about you. Thinking about what it'd be like to do so much more than merely kiss you. Wanting to touch you in places that would make you groan again. But he didn't say that.

"No." She reared back to look at him. "It's so much more than that."

She felt it, too, then, he realized. She felt the emotions building between them. It wasn't just sexual attraction.

"Claire," he said, cupping her jaw again, and she didn't move away. No, she tipped her head so that she pressed her cheek into his palm, like a contented cat. He grew brave then, bent to kiss her again. She watched his head lower. He saw her pupils dilate in anticipation, but she didn't move away. When their lips connected, she kissed him back and he knew what he wanted then. It wasn't just to be with her. He wanted to be one with her. To love her. To bring her joy and pleasure and happiness as she'd never known before. It was a need as fierce as the one he'd felt to fight for his country.

"Where's your bedroom?"

She pointed behind them. Her cheeks were flushed. Her eyes were soft and she was the sexiest damn thing he'd ever seen.

"Let's go."

Chapter Fifteen

What was she doing?

You're going to have sex.

The answer was as clear and as simple and as firm as that. She was going to go to bed with Ethan McCall and she wasn't going to regret it. She was going to revel in what it felt like to be touched by a man once again because, damn it all, it'd been far too long.

"Do you have protection?" he asked, stopping by the side of her bed.

"No." She'd had no need of birth control, not when she didn't plan on sleeping with anyone. "Do you?"

He shook his head.

She didn't want to get pregnant, although as she did the mental math she figured she should be okay. Still, that wasn't the point. It mattered.

She just didn't care.

Her whole body tingled. Not just the center of her. Everything, everywhere, all over. She wanted him and the release that would come from being with him and damn the consequences.

"I guess I should ask if I need to be worried about you."

He shook his head. "I've been overseas for months, and I don't make a habit of using my leave to chase down women. It's been a long time for me, too."

The confession, coming as it did from such a handsome man, should have surprised her. Somehow it didn't. He didn't seem the type to mess around. He seemed the type to want to care first.

"Then I guess I'm not worried."

"Good," he said, his hand reaching out and sliding under her shirt. She didn't wear a bra. Had he known that? If he didn't he knew it now because her nipples contracted the moment his fingers brushed her belly. The tingling turned into ripples of pleasure, and she closed her eyes as she allowed him to touch her, all of her, her shirt sliding off her shoulders with her barely noticing.

"I've been wanting to kiss you like this for days."

She felt the brush of his breath, knew what he was about to do and arched into him in anticipation because the ripples had intensified. Something soft yet sharp captured the tip of her and she moaned.

"Just like this," he said, circling her with his tongue.

Somehow she found herself backed up against the bed although she had no idea if he'd guided her there or if she'd moved. He kept kissing her, though, and it made her grow weak at the knees to the point that she sank onto the bed. He didn't follow her down. He simply stared at her and the look in his eyes made her feel so sexy and so wanted that she didn't hesitate to unsnap her jeans, and then lower the zipper. Her underwear followed the pants. He did the same, first pulling his shirt out of the waistband of his jeans, then unbuttoning his pink shirt. She'd never seen him so naked before and she realized then how fit a body he had. The wounds on his arms had long since healed, but they did nothing to detract from the physical splendor that was Ethan.

He drew his jeans down next, kneeling to pull them over his feet, which had been stripped of their boots at some point although she didn't recall him taking them off.

"Slip on over," he said softly.

It was the moment of truth. They were both

naked, and once she moved he would be on the bed with her. This wonderful, glorious man would make love to her. It would be only the second time she'd been with a man since Marcus.

Don't think about that.

He slid down next to her, on his belly, his shoulders so wide and so big she found herself reaching out and touching them. He touched her, too, her face, swiping a lock of hair off her cheek.

"So beautiful," he said.

No, she wasn't. Her nose was too big and her mouth too wide. She hated how little her breasts were and she felt as if she had monster thighs.

He didn't appear to notice. No. He looked into her eyes, not at her body.

"So very, very beautiful," he said.

He talked about her soul. It melted her heart in a way that made her eyes warm with tears. That was the last thought she had before the ripples of pleasure took over again, and desire replaced thought because he leaned toward her and kissed her. She opened her mouth to him immediately and it all became a jumble. His hand on her thigh. Her tongue brushing his lips. His fingers trailing a path to her center. She didn't want him to wait, but he took his time. His mouth moved off her own, soft lips brushing her neck and then her collarbone, his hand cupping her and causing her to cry out in pleasure. He worked her like a master craftsman, her body clay in his hands as he molded her and touched her and turned her desire into a frenzy.

"Ethan."

He must have heard the frustration in her voice because he moved. She felt his knee nudge her and she didn't hesitate as she welcomed him home.

"Oh, sweet heaven," she thought she heard him mutter.

He filled her perfectly and she thought she

might die of pleasure right there and then, but he refused to hurry. She tried to edge him on, lifted her hips, pressed him down into her, and yet he took her gently and slowly and she wanted to cry all over again at how perfect it all felt.

Her soft sighs turned into moans and her moans into cries of pleasure. Her hips matched his slow rhythm and it was as if they'd been together before. He knew exactly how to move and when to slow down and when to speed up and as she drew closer and closer to her breaking point, he knew when to let her go.

"Claire," he cried out.

She followed the sound of his voice, landing on the sweet side of pleasure, her cry of release so loud she knew she should feel shame. No, she silently amended as she slowly drifted back into the reality of his arms, not shame. Wonder. And delight. And something else she couldn't identify, a something that caused a sharp jolt of fear, but she thrust that something back down before it could take over her thoughts. What she wanted right now was to hold Ethan. To sleep for a while held in a man's arms. She'd missed that for so long.

"Here," he said, shifting so that she could move to the side and he could hold her tight.

"Thank you."

Is that what you say to men these days? she wondered. What was the protocol after you'd just had mind-blowing sex with someone you'd met less than two months ago? She didn't know, and at that moment, she didn't care. Her lids grew heavy and she didn't want to fight the sleep that tried to claim her. For once in her life she didn't want to fight at all. She was tired of doing battle. She wanted to rest and to be held and to feel as if she hadn't a care in the world.

So she slept.

And Ethan held her. He doubted she felt him kiss the top of her head. Knew she had no idea that he drew back a bit and stared into her face, studying her, memorizing her.

What am I going to do with you? he silently asked. *You're going to fight this. I know you are.*

But he was a soldier, a warrior. Someone who didn't fear combat, even when the war about to be waged was simply a battle to win a woman's heart.

SHE DREAMED SHE was at the ocean and Marcus, no, Ethan was there with her. They were frolicking in the ocean and water lapped at her calves.

She awoke with a start.

Ethan still held her. His toes were twitching as he slept, his legs entwined with hers so that she felt the movement on the back of her leg. It was daylight outside.

Adam.

She had no idea when he'd be home this morning. In the old days, back when she'd had "date night" with Marcus and Chance had been out on leave her brother wouldn't bring him back without calling first. But it'd been a while since she and Adam had been apart and she wondered if he'd miss her and what he'd say if he knew Ethan had spent the night.

That she couldn't deal with right now. Right now she needed to get up and get dressed. But first shower. Definitely shower.

She moved slowly, for some reason not wanting to awaken Ethan. No. That wasn't true. She didn't want to talk right now. She needed time to absorb what had just happened, to figure out where it left her and what it might mean. He'd been such a tender and gentle lover. At one point she'd found herself crying at the beauty of it all, but looming in the back of her mind, always there in the after moments, were thoughts about the morning and what would happen then.

Somehow she managed to extricate herself without him noticing. She scurried to the bathroom, listening for signs that he'd awoken as she waited for the water to warm. She caught a glimpse of herself in the mirror, fingered her swollen lips, tried to straighten her wild hair, checked to make sure there were no marks on the side of her neck where the scruff of his chin had rubbed her raw, or so it had seemed. She saw no evidence of their lovemaking.

So she showered to help clear her mind. She emerged from it feeling grateful that if Adam arrived home now, she would be reasonably presentable. Of course, there was the matter of the sleeping man in her bed.

She attempted to rectify that problem the moment she pulled on clothes. Goodness knew why, but she tiptoed to the bedside, about to shake him awake when she paused to simply stare. He appeared to be dreaming, and not a good dream, either, based on the way he twitched and flicked his head from side to side. She watched, wondering if she should wake him. Clearly that was what he suffered from, because his movements became more jerky and more frantic until she couldn't stop herself.

"Ethan."

Green eyes popped open. They instantly found hers, his face going from frightened to puzzled to understanding.

"Damn." He quickly sat up, and then shifted so he sat on the side of the bed. "Thanks."

"Are you okay?"

He rested his elbows on his knees, rubbed his temple. "Nightmare."

"Figured as much."

"What time is it?"

"Seven." He nodded and she wondered if he had bad dreams on a regular basis. "I was going to wake you up anyway. I'm not sure what time Adam will be back."

He scrubbed the sleep out of his eyes and she found that gesture adorable. "Yeah. Good. I should probably get a move on."

He started to stand and she retreated like a frightened cat. He froze for a moment and she realized he'd noticed, but didn't say anything.

She turned away, murmuring, "I'll make breakfast." Something about the terror she'd glimpsed in his eyes tore at her heart. He wasn't over his time in the Middle East. Not by a long shot. "There's a fresh towel in the bathroom. Feel free to use my shampoo and whatever else you want."

She called the words out over her shoulder because she didn't want to see him standing there naked. It seemed so silly to be suddenly shy around him, not after all they'd done, but it was different this morning. Last night had been magical. Today, reality.

Which leaves you exactly where? she asked herself.

She didn't know. Didn't want to think about it. Breakfast first. Then maybe she'd be able to think clearer.

He entered the kitchen as she was sliding fried eggs onto plates. The toast was already done and the smell of bacon filled the air. Once upon a time he'd cooked for her. Funny. That seemed like a lifetime ago.

"I could get used to this," he said as he took a seat. And he looked better. More himself. Less shaky. He still had his five-o'clock shadow and she was struck by the notion once again of just how much he looked like a younger version of George Clooney with his salt-and-pepper hair.

"Mom!"

She froze. Ethan didn't. He just took the plate and sat down at the table.

"Mo-om."

"In here," she called back.

Adam arrived at the doorway to the kitchen, looking adorable and a little boyish with a crooked smile on his face that melted her heart. To her utter shock, he didn't bat an eye when he spotted Ethan sitting at the table, just said, "I'm hungry. What's to eat?"

She froze with her own plate in her hand. "I, um…" Ethan caught her gaze, smiled. "I just made fried eggs."

"Yum." He went to the kitchen table and sat down. "Uncle Colt only had cereal at his place. I was hungry for real food. Natalie offered to make it for me, but she only does the scrambled eggs and I don't like that."

She almost laughed. It was as if Ethan wasn't even there. No. That wasn't right. Her son smiled in the man's direction. "Hey, Ethan."

"Mornin', Adam."

"Can I have a fried egg, Mom?"

"Sure." She handed her son her own plate. "I'll make another."

"Cool."

And that was that. No funny looks. No curious comments. No awkward questions.

The knot in her stomach eased a bit.

Of course he might think Ethan had arrived early in the morning, as he often did. Her son probably had no idea he'd spent the night. That made more sense than anything else. She'd been worried over nothing.

Her son munched on a strip of bacon. "The rodeo was awesome. Colt said I can do it again at another rodeo if I want."

She didn't know what to say other than, "Oh. Well, yeah. I guess."

"Gonna ride Playboy again later today." Her son looked up. "If that's okay with you."

There it was again, the familiar urge to tell him no, to hand him the excuse that he was too weak or not ready or unable to handle the physical exertion. It was hard, but she somehow managed to say, "That sounds fine."

She was rewarded with a smile that made her throat tighten.

"Why don't we all go riding?" Ethan said.

"Yeah." Adam gobbled down another bite, then said, "Can we, Mom?"

Claire looked up. She shot Ethan a look that clearly expressed her opinion of the idea, and it wasn't favorable. Ethan just smiled, and oddly, she suddenly wanted to smile, too. Wretch.

"After we feed the dogs and work Thor," Ethan said.

"Cool. I'll go text Uncle Colt."

He was off like a shot, and Claire was surprised to realize he'd finished his breakfast. He left silence behind, but it was comfortable and Claire didn't mind because she was able to finish her own breakfast, Ethan watching her take every bite. It was both erotic and annoying to feel his gaze upon her, but she did her best not to let him see.

"You don't have to go with us if you don't want to," he said when she finished.

"No." She set her dishes in the sink. "I can tolerate riding one more time."

He nodded, smiled. "Good. Why don't you meet me in an hour or so? That'll give me time to finish my chores for your brother, too."

"Sounds good."

"I was actually wanting to take Thor on a ride, if that's okay, to test him. See if he's ready for the big outdoors. I figure if he runs I have a better shot at catching him on a horse."

"You probably would."

"So you're okay with that?"

"Of course."

"Good." He got up, and before she could say another word, pinned her to the counter with his arms on either side. "I'll see you later, then."

The ripples struck with a force that left her breathless. "Later," she echoed.

She thought he would kiss her, but he didn't. Instead he brushed his lips against her neck. Just a light touch but it was enough to make her knees weak.

He left her standing there, wilting against the

countertop. She heard him leave the house, saw him head toward the kennels out of her kitchen window. She felt herself move then. She didn't recall making the decision to watch him, but she did, smiling at the way Thor spotted him the minute he stepped outside, and the way the dog got up and headed toward the entrance. A minute later they both emerged, Thor's tail wagging, a canine grin on his face.

The dog worshipped Ethan. It was so obvious. Equally obvious was Ethan's affection for Thor. He reached down, scrubbed a hand through his fur, playfully grabbed an ear. Thor loved it. She watched the two and just smiled.

She could love Ethan.

The thought landed like a brick. She staggered back from the counter.

"Mom. What's wrong?"

She turned away from the window, wiped a tear from her eyes she hadn't even known had fallen. "Nothing, kiddo."

"Did Ethan leave?"

"He's outside working with Thor, but he said to meet him in about an hour."

"I'm going outside to help him, then."

"Sure."

But her son stared at her funny. "I like him, Mom."

She wasn't going to say anything, just nod, but instead she heard herself say, "I like him, too, honey."

And it scared the hell out of her.

Chapter Sixteen

His cell phone rang the moment he entered his apartment above the barn. It startled him because he'd forgotten he had the thing with him.

"Dr. Ethan McCall?" asked a voice after he answered.

"Affirmative," Ethan answered, the response automatic after all his years in the military.

"This is Lance Kittrick."

It took him a moment to place the name, and when he did, he jerked upright. "Mr. Kittrick, it's an honor."

The man was a legend in the world of combat dogs. One of the few known breeders of Belgian

Malinois in the States. His training facility in Montana was world-renowned, too—police officers, military personnel and private contractors were regular customers. He'd applied there on a whim even though he knew they kept a veterinarian on retainer already, but he'd thought maybe he could get his foot in the door, to do what he really wanted to do, which was get into the business of breeding and training military dogs. He could learn from the best while still practicing medicine, move in with his parents if he had to.

"Actually, the honor's all mine, Major."

"Not major anymore, sir. It's just Dr. McCall."

"Well, Dr. McCall, we were glad to receive your résumé."

He'd sent out a bunch when he'd arrived at the ranch, back before he'd realized how much living at Misfit Farms suited him. And now with Claire in his life…

"Yes, sir. About that. My situation has changed.

I'm working for a farm and I'm not going to lie, I'd like to stay here."

For as long as Claire would have him. With any luck, she felt the same way, too.

"Really?" said Mr. Kittrick. "That's too bad. Your résumé came at the perfect time. Our staff veterinarian has decided he'd like to retire and so we're starting to put out feelers for a new one. With your military experience and connections, you'd be a perfect addition to our outfit."

He wouldn't be human if he didn't feel a twinge of regret. What were the odds that he'd be offered his dream job at this point in his life? When he'd first gotten back home he'd have jumped at the chance; now all he did was hold on to the phone tighter. It was a dream job, but he couldn't take it. It would mean leaving Claire…

"When would you be looking to hire someone?"

"Soon, and before you say no again, why don't

I fly you out here so you can look over the place? I think you'd be pleased with what we've got. Plus, your cover letter said you wanted to learn how to train."

"Yes, sir. I know the basics, but I've never done it professionally."

"Well, son, that's our specialty, as I'm sure you know." The man paused to let his words sink in. "Look, I'm not going to lie. When I got your résumé I put it aside, thinking if something came up we'd give you a call. I had no idea our doc was thinking of retiring. He'd mentioned it but I didn't think he meant right away. Took me by surprise last week when he sat me down and broke the news, but then I thought about your résumé. You're my first call."

He took a deep breath, glanced out the window, at Misfit Farms and the horses in the pasture and the way the sun made the mountains in the distance look like something an artist would paint.

"Can I get back to you?"

"Sure, sure," Mr. Kittrick said. "Why don't you think about it for a couple days? I'll hold off making any more phone calls until I hear back from you."

He released the breath. "I'd appreciate that, sir."

When he hung up he realized his hands were shaking again, but for a different reason this time. Come to think of it, he hadn't felt anxious in over a week. He had Claire to thank for that. She'd shown him the true meaning of bravery in the face of adversity. Yes, he'd lost his best friend, but like Claire, he would stand strong.

He couldn't leave her.

Still, when Claire showed up with Adam and Thor in tow, his mind was a million miles away. What would it hurt if he flew out there and took a look? There was nothing wrong with a long-distance relationship. It would mean making adjustments, but if anyone could handle the strain of an out-of-state boyfriend, it would be Claire. She'd been a military wife.

"Thor, hey," he said, greeting the dog. Not that the animal could hear him but he was pretty certain Thor could read the expression on his face and maybe even his mouth. "Ready?"

"I hope he doesn't run away," Claire said.

"He won't."

"Let's go!" Adam shouted, running to the pasture where his horse was kept.

"He's been like this all morning."

Ethan nodded, motioning for Thor to sit. "He likes riding."

"He likes swimming even better and that's what he plans to do once he gets to the stock pond."

Did he tell her? Or should he keep the news to himself? He honestly didn't know.

"I'll go get your horse," he offered.

"No. It's okay. You've got Thor. I can get Blue myself."

He didn't argue. Plus, keeping busy gave him time to think. Thor followed him to his horse's side. He worried about how the dog would react with the horse, but Thor hung back as Ethan went to work brushing and saddling. When he emerged from the barn a few moments later he was happy to see Thor following. The dog never took his eyes off him.

"Where'd you put your swim trunks?" he was just in time to hear Claire ask Adam.

"In here." Adam pointed to saddlebags he must have found in the tack room.

"You ready?" she asked Ethan next.

"Let's go."

Claire mounted up and so did Ethan, and when he was on board, he motioned for Thor to heel. The dog didn't hesitate.

"That's a good sign."

Ethan nodded. Thor would be okay. He cued his horse to move forward. Adam rode up alongside him and he was like a different kid, Ethan noticed. The boy he'd been when Ethan had arrived had still been recovering from cancer treatment. This boy was alive and well and full of youthful enthusiasm.

"Thor sure is behaving," the boy observed.

"He is."

Who would work with the dog if he left?

"What's wrong?" Claire asked, riding up to him.

How had she so easily gleaned that the thought of leaving Thor, of leaving them all, had him distracted? He inhaled deeply, trying to clear his thoughts. The familiar scent of leather and horse should be a comfort to him, but it wasn't. It was both a comfort and a curse because it was yet another reminder of what he would miss if he left. No more horseback rides with Claire.

"Ethan?"

Adam seemed oblivious. The boy was already halfway to the gate.

"I had a phone call just before you arrived."

She sat up straighter in the saddle. "What kind of call?"

He clucked his horse forward so they were side by side. "From a potential employer. In Montana."

Her face actually twitched as if she'd been hit. "You're leaving?"

"Just for a few days." It wasn't until that moment that he realized he wanted to go and at least check out the place. "I'll be there and back before you know it."

"Come on, you guys." They both turned to Adam, who waited by the gate. He waved them forward. "We don't got all day."

Claire clucked her horse forward, and he knew she wasn't happy, but he really couldn't blame her. The whole scope of their relationship had changed last night and here he was less than twenty-four hours later talking about leaving.

"It's just a quick trip."

She nodded, but she wouldn't look at him. "So you're considering the job, then?"

"No. Well, maybe. I don't know."

"And what about your commitment to my brother and his wife?"

He glanced at Thor to ensure the dog was still with him. He was. "That was always just a temporary thing."

"So you've never planned on sticking around?"

"It's not like I'm saying yes to the job."

"But you're considering it."

He felt as if he was back on the front lines, afraid of making a wrong step and potentially blowing everything up. "I think it's smart to keep my options open."

"So you *are* considering it?"

Okay. This conversation was going nowhere fast. He wished he could change the subject, except he knew he'd never get away with that.

"Claire, I can't keep mooching off your brother."

She pulled her horse up. "You're not mooching. Just the other day he was saying what a big help you are around here. Not only that, but you've made it clear you're happy here, that you were considering staying."

He stopped, too, making sure Thor did the same. The dog instantly sat near his horse's shoulder. "I'm a veterinarian, not a stable boy."

"And you'll be doing veterinarian work once you start Misfit Farm's breeding program."

"That's just looking through a microscope and palpating mares, and dealing with a single stallion. Honestly, a vet tech could do that."

"And what about that offer from Mariah Johnson? She was hoping you could cover for her while she's out on maternity leave."

"That's months away. She has plenty of time to find someone else."

"So you really are leaving, then."

"I don't know!" He hadn't meant to say the words so loud, but a quick glance at Adam revealed the kid's eyes were wide. He stood by the gate, watching the adults, a frown quickly replacing his smile.

"You've done the long-distance relationship thing before, Claire. I didn't think it'd be a big deal if I proposed the same idea now."

She glanced at Ethan, too, and he had to strain to hear her when she said, "Is that what we're in? A relationship?"

He didn't like the way she said the words, nor the look on her face. It wasn't that she was angry, it was more that she seemed hurt, so much so that he softened his own voice. "Of course it is."

He saw her hands tighten on the reins. She stared straight ahead and suddenly all he wanted to do was pull her into his arms, except he couldn't.

"I was young when I first met Marcus. Too young. I honestly think part of my attraction to him was that he could take me away from all this." She motioned with her hand toward the farm. "But now I'm older and I like my life and I love where I live. I could never leave this ranch."

"I'm not asking you to."

"And I don't know that I'm willing to be in a relationship with someone who lives halfway across the country. I would want more."

Adam must have sensed the need for the two adults to have some privacy because he left the gate open and started to ride on. Ethan was surprised Claire didn't call him back, but maybe she didn't notice. She stared down at her saddle and she seemed so sad all of a sudden that he shifted his weight and placed a hand on her thigh.

"It's just a scouting mission. I may not even like the place."

"And if you do? What then?"

"We'll talk about it."

She lifted her head, watched her son ride off,

and Ethan could see the play of emotions on her face. She took a deep breath and he saw the sadness deepen and in that moment he wanted to pull the words back, to unsay what he'd said, to ease her pain, except he couldn't.

"You know, when I first met you I didn't want to like you." Her thumb absently toyed with her reins. "I was attracted to you right from the get-go. Getting involved with you scared the hell out of me."

"I know."

"But you want to know what scares me more?" She turned and pinned him with a stare. "The thought of you leaving."

"Claire—"

"No." She lifted a hand. "Let me finish. I care for you, Ethan. After last night, I'm no longer in denial. I'm not the type to jump into bed with someone without it meaning something afterward. And you're right. I was a military wife once before, but I met and married Marcus while he was in the States. It happened fast." She smiled wryly. "I'm starting to think that's a habit of mine. I don't fall slow and easy. I fall hard."

What was she saying?

"But I'm older and wiser now. I know what I want, and a long-distance relationship isn't it."

He knew what she tried to tell him then. If he stayed she would commit to him 100 percent. And if he didn't…

"It wouldn't be like I was in the military," he felt the need to point out. "I'd be able to fly back and forth on a regular basis. You'd be able to come and see me."

"And who would take care of my place?"

He glanced at the house to their left. "Your brother."

She shook her head. "I've had enough of that. My brother probably has, too. No, Ethan. A long-distance relationship won't work for me.

Not anymore. I'm too old for that. Too set in my ways. It's me or…"

Nothing.

She didn't need to say the word. He understood. But he wasn't going to argue. It might all be a moot point. He just wanted to go look. To meet a man who was a legend in the military dog world. And if something happened and he ended up wanting to take the job, he would have to change her mind.

He just wasn't certain he could.

Chapter Seventeen

He left two days later. Ethan didn't know it, but she watched him drive away. She'd taken Thor out, had walked the dog far away so that he couldn't see them standing there, watching from the line of trees.

"He'll be back," she told Thor, who whined. He knew his master was leaving. She didn't know how he knew. It wasn't as if he could hear the sound of Ethan's car. Or that he even knew what car Ethan drove since he walked over most of the time. Yet somehow the dog knew his favorite human had left.

She walked back the long way around. And

even though it was a weekday, Misfit Farms was a hive of activity. Natalie had an assistant trainer working for her now, a former student who'd gone on to success in the hunter/jumper world, and Laney waved hello when she spotted her walking past.

"Hey, Claire," she called, pulling up the horse she schooled next to the rail in the covered arena. "You're up early."

She waved back. "Needed some fresh air."

"Claire," someone called to her right. She turned to see Natalie standing at the entrance to the barn. Colt was there, too, the couple waving her over. "We were just talking about you," Natalie added.

Uh-oh. That boded ill. Colt had a sixth sense when it came to her emotions. There'd been so many times when they'd been growing up when their dad had been cruel to her in some small way and Colt had come home just knowing.

"Do you have a second?" Colt asked.

"Sure," she said with a glance down at Thor. The dog's big ears were aimed at Natalie, as if he tried to hear her words, and when he couldn't he glanced up at her. "Come," she mouthed, motioning with her hand for him to heel.

Her brother and Natalie had an office overlooking the covered arena. She entered the Western-themed room and marveled at how much had changed in the space of a year. They had pictures of Laney, the teen with a passion for horses, on the wall. She'd grown six inches since Natalie had started working with her, making her the perfect big equitation rider, which Natalie claimed was a gift from the gods. There was win photo after win photo on the wall, all mixed in with pictures of Colt and Natalie riding.

"Sit down."

The feeling that something serious was about to be said only intensified. She took a seat on the leather couch that hugged the same wall as the one the door was set into. They leaned against the edge of the oak desk that took up the other wall.

"Will I need a stiff drink?" she asked.

Natalie and Colt exchanged glances. Those gazes held for a moment and she watched as the look on Natalie's face softened in a way she'd never seen before. And even though they were both in profile, she clearly saw the gleam of excitement in their eyes. It was Natalie who turned toward her and said softly, gently, "We're pregnant."

And Claire just sat there, dumbfounded, the word repeating over and over in her head. "Pregnant?" she repeated.

Natalie nodded.

"Oh, my goodness, are you serious?"

Colt nodded this time, and Claire couldn't breathe. No. That wasn't true. She could breathe. It was just her throat was thick with tears.

Happy tears, she told herself, and she was happy. Thrilled.

"That's great, you guys." She wiped at her eyes. "I'm so happy for you."

Natalie and Colt exchanged glances.

"We wanted to wait to catch you alone," Natalie said. "So you could tell Adam in your own way. We weren't sure how he would take the news."

"Are you kidding? He'll be thrilled." And the tears kept coming. In fact, she had to work to regulate her breathing because all of a sudden, she felt like sobbing. "That's amazing news."

"Then why are you crying?" Colt asked.

She thought about playing dumb, but she'd never been anything but honest with her brother and sister-in-law. "I don't know."

And then she did bawl. She bawled like a baby, which was horrible because they'd just shared some fantastic news and she felt as if she'd just lost her best friend and she had no idea why.

"Claire," her brother said gently. She hadn't even noticed when he'd moved to stand in front of her. "What is it, sis? Is it Adam? Did a blood test reveal some bad news?"

She shook her head, so blinded by her tears she had to keep wiping at her eyes. "No." And the word had come out sounding like a wail and she was mortified because she had never, not once in all the years, sounded so pitiful. Not when Marcus had come back from the Middle East sick. Not when she'd realized he was going to die. Not even when Adam had been diagnosed with cancer.

What was wrong with her?

"Maybe you two should have a moment alone."

"No, stay," she said, grabbing Natalie's hand as she tried to pass. Her sister-in-law's face was a mask of concern and it was humiliating, because this wasn't about Claire. This should be about her brother and his wife.

"I'm thrilled for you," she said. "I really am. I can't wait to be an aunt." She hoped they saw how sincerely she meant the words, because she knew there was a time when Colt didn't even want children. The fact that he was expecting his first child, and that he clearly brimmed with pride over the whole thing, was a sign of how much he loved his wife and what a beautiful marriage they had.

"We know you're happy for us," Natalie said gently.

Claire scrubbed at her eyes again. "It's just been one of those days."

"Is it because Ethan left?" Colt asked. "Is that why you're crying?"

"No," she said quickly, emphatically. "This has nothing to do with that."

"Did you fall in love with him?" Natalie asked.

"No. Of course not." How could she fall in

love with a man in a matter of weeks? "It's not like that."

Her brother and his wife exchanged glances again, and it was Colt who said, "Are you sure?"

"Well, I mean I'm sad that he's gone. But he'll be back."

But she knew how much he wanted to train dogs. It was a big deal that he'd been invited east to meet Lance Kittrick. Even she knew who the man was. She wouldn't blame him if he *did* want to leave and take a job with him. She was just sad, was all, sad that he'd be moving on.

Because you've fallen for him.

No, she firmly told herself. She cared for him deeply, but love? No.

"What will you do if he wants the job?" Natalie asked.

"What do you mean what will I do?" She had better control of herself now. The tears had faded, thank God. "Nothing. He needs to make his own choices."

Choices that wouldn't involve her. That was what made her sad. She'd thought they were headed someplace with their relationship, but then the very first time he'd been offered an opportunity to leave, he'd jumped at it. It hurt, damn it. She wouldn't lie to herself.

"Congratulations," she said, getting up and hugging Natalie. Hard. "Really. I can't wait to hold my new niece or nephew." She hugged her brother next, only he didn't let her go.

"I love you, sis," she heard him say.

She got weepy again. "I know."

"I'm here if you need me."

"I know. Thanks." But she didn't need any man. She'd just forgotten that, but she remembered it now. It was something she would not forget, not ever again.

HE DROVE HOME SLOWLY.

Home.

Funny how that was what he called Misfit

Farms in his head. Was it home? He couldn't deny that as he pulled into the main drive he felt his heart accelerate. He wanted to see Claire, to share with her the details of his trip, to tell her how much of a thrill it'd been to meet Lance Kittrick and to tour his state-of-the-art ranch.

He drove straight to her place. She wasn't home, though, her van missing from the driveway. Thor was glad to see him. He could hear the dog's cries from Claire's front yard and their reunion a few seconds later solidified in Ethan's head that he wanted to adopt the dog. He'd been meaning to talk to Claire about it for a few weeks now, had meant to tell her about it on the day of that disastrous trail ride. But she'd clammed up on him after he'd broken the news about his potential job offer and the timing hadn't felt right. He would rectify that situation the moment he saw her, he vowed, bending down and scratching Thor's thick, black head. He'd missed the dog. Missed this place.

Missed Claire.

He wasn't going to take the job. He wanted to. Lord, how he wanted to, but his absence from the ranch had made him realize just how much he loved the place.

"What do you think, boy? You think I should stick around?"

Thor tried to lick his face. He smiled and scratched his head. He hung out for a little while longer; put Thor through his paces. He half hoped Claire would show up, and when she didn't, he reluctantly put Thor away. He thought maybe she might be over at her brother's, but she wasn't there, either.

"She went to go pick up another dog," Colt explained the next morning when Ethan arrived to help him feed. "She won't be back until to-morrow."

Was it his imagination, or was the look on Colt's face one of disappointment? It'd dawned a chilly morning thanks to coastal fog that had reached its smudgy gray fingers inland, but the cold in the barn aisle was echoed in Colt's eyes.

"Really?" he asked curiously. "I'm surprised she didn't mention it to me."

"Why would she, when she wasn't even sure you were coming back?"

Ethan almost flinched at the sharpness of Colt's words. "Is that what she said?"

"No," Colt admitted.

Clearly, that was what everyone thought. "I'm not going to move to Montana."

Some of the animosity faded. "You're not."

"I thought about it, but in the end California has something Montana doesn't."

"What's that?"

"Your sister."

Colt's face went completely still, but then he smiled a bit, a wry kind of smile but also one tinged by approval. "I'm glad to hear that."

"I care too much for your sister to leave."

"Good, because I'm pretty sure she's halfway in love with you."

Ethan tipped his head because he couldn't have heard him right. "What?"

"She won't admit it. Cried like a baby right there in the office that day you left."

"She did?"

Colt nodded. "Told us she was 'just emotional,' which I know she was." And then Colt's smile took on the intensity of headlights. "My wife is pregnant."

Ethan didn't even hesitate. He moved forward, held out his hand. "Wow, man. That's awesome."

"Yes, it is." Colt's swiped a hand through his dark hair. "We weren't really trying, either, so it's a little surreal."

"You're going to be a great dad."

Colt's smile lost some of its luster. "I just hope I can be half the parent my sister is."

"Adam's a great kid."

"She would do anything to protect him."

"I know."

"She deserves to be happy."

"She's the reason I came back to California."

"Just make sure she knows that."

Chapter Eighteen

It was a good trip, Claire told herself repeatedly as she drove through Via Del Caballo's darkened streets. She'd picked up another dog to re-home and she'd dropped off a dog to a new family. That was the best part of her job and the reason she'd pulled every string she knew to become one of the rare kennels in the United States approved to re-home MWDs.

Marcus would be proud.

She tried not to think about Marcus and the shame she felt at having slept with Ethan. That was why she'd been such an emotional wreck the other day. She'd slept with a man and she'd had feelings afterward, serious feelings, and she didn't know what to do about that.

Colt had told her Ethan was back. Of course, she'd known that. He'd texted her and called. She'd ignored him. Colt had also told her Ethan had said he didn't want the job back in Montana, something she was pretty sure Ethan wanted to tell her himself. She hadn't given him the chance. She should have been relieved. Happy. Thrilled. Instead she felt scared, anxious and upset.

"Mom, I'm tired," Adam muttered sleepily as they passed between the electronic gates.

That was the other bit of good news. While they'd been down south, they'd seen his oncologist. Adam had had another blood test and scans, and the results had been good. Zero cancer cells. Normal white blood cell levels. No growths. No evidence of disease, the doctor had said.

Remission.

It was within their reach. Oh, he would still need to see his oncologist on a regular basis, but those visits would get further and further apart until he wouldn't have to go at all. Eventually. A long time in his future.

The future.

She didn't want to think about that, or the fact that Ethan was back at the ranch, and that she would have to talk to him and tell him—

What?

She felt her eyes begin to fill with tears all over again, and it made her mad because she had nothing, absolutely nothing to cry about and yet that was all she'd been doing since he'd left for Montana. Lord, she still couldn't believe she'd turned into a blubbering fool when Colt had told her they were expecting a child. She'd completely humiliated herself, and she felt horribly guilty because the news should have been a joyous occasion and instead she'd acted like a crazy woman.

Somehow she got Adam into bed without waking him. It meant carrying him to his room and forcing him into his jammies before tucking him beneath the sheets, the new dog she'd brought home having to wait in the back of the van. Since it was night outside and cool, she didn't worry. Instead she took a moment to observe Adam's sweet, innocent face illuminated by the night-light in the corner of his Hawkman-themed bedroom.

Remission.

His blood work was news that should make her cry, except it didn't. She hadn't even told Colt or Chance yet.

With a kiss on the forehead she headed back outside. The new dog greeted her with a canine smile and a wag of his tail.

"Come here, Fido."

That was really the dog's name. A joke on the part of the breeder, no doubt, but it didn't make her smile. Not tonight.

She went to work, switching on the kennel lights, making sure the new dog had water. Watching, once she turned Fido loose in Janus's old kennel, to make sure he got along with the other dogs. When she was done, she went up to the animal.

"I hope you enjoy your new digs." She patted the dog's head. "We'll have you in an even-better home in no time."

She'd re-homed a lot of dogs in recent weeks. It was a crazy process. Online applications, background checks, references. The dogs, too, needed to be prepped. Health check. Spayed or neutered if that wasn't done already. Travel arrangements. She could have had the whole place emptied out if she wasn't so picky about matching the right human with the right dog. Sometimes she had a person come back two or three times before she agreed to the adoption. Sometimes it was just once—like Naomi.

Naomi.

The woman had sent her a video of her kids' reaction when Janus had arrived. It'd made her bawl like a baby all over again. If she didn't know better she would swear she was pregnant, but she knew for a fact she didn't have to worry about that.

The dogs grew restless, but that was to be expected given they'd just been introduced to a new roommate. One of them started to bark. Then another.

"Lass das sein," scolded a voice.

Silence. She could hear his footfalls then, turned and sure enough, there he was.

Ethan.

"Hey," she all but croaked.

"You're back," he said.

"What are you doing here?" She didn't mean to be rude, but he was the last person she'd expected to see this time of night.

"I saw the headlights on the road."

Had he? She didn't think that was possible, but she wasn't going to argue.

"It's late," she said, hoping he would take the hint.

"Why haven't you returned my texts or my calls?"

She lifted her chin. "What was there to say? Whatever your decision, it was yours to make, not mine."

"I'm not leaving."

"I know. Colt told me."

He appeared puzzled. "Then why didn't you want to talk to me?"

This was the conversation she'd been hoping to have tomorrow. The one that she'd known would be hard. The reason she'd been crying, she finally admitted.

"Because I didn't want to tell you that, go or stay, California or Montana, it wouldn't matter in the end." She took a deep breath. "I can't do this, Ethan. I can't…" She searched for the right words, the words she'd been hoping she'd have a whole night to find before facing him. "I can't be in a relationship."

"Why the hell not?"

Great. And now he was angry, only that wasn't the look in his eyes. No. He seemed determined.

"I don't want to hurt…" *Me. I don't want to be terrified of losing you. I can't face another loss.* "Adam," she said instead. "He's still so fragile healthwise. I need to focus on him."

It was a bunch of bunk. He'd be fine. At last she had started to believe that, and if she didn't miss her guess, Ethan thought so, too.

"You're a coward."

She jerked upright. "I am not."

"All this time I thought you were so brave, but in the end, you can't face the truth."

"What truth?"

"You're afraid of falling in love."

"No, I'm not."

"You are. I can see it in your eyes."

"Okay, fine. Maybe I am."

He took a step toward her. She told herself not to retreat. She needed to stay strong. This was for the best. "It's going to be okay," he said, resting his hands on his shoulder. "You're not going to lose me."

"I'm not afraid of that."

Aren't you? Isn't that exactly what's wrong?

"Then why are you pushing me away?"

"Because it won't work out," she finally admitted. "Because my life is too crazy." Lord, it felt good to say the words out loud. "Because we hardly know each other. Because I have a son who has a tender heart and he'll fall in love with you, too, and when it all falls apart, he'll be hurt in the process."

"No," he said with a shake of his head. "It won't fall apart. Have some faith."

"Faith." She huffed in derision. "I had faith my husband would get better, and look where that got me."

He drew back, clearly surprised by the venom in her voice, but it felt good to let that out, too.

"I had faith that nothing else bad would happen, but look at Adam."

"He's getting better."

She ignored his words. "And before that. I had faith that my dad would change. That he would stop beating the crap out of me and my brothers, but he never changed. Even at the bitter end he was just as coldhearted and mean as he always was. You know what he said to me just before he died?" She swallowed back a lump of emotion in her throat. "He said maybe if I'd taken better care of my husband he wouldn't have died."

It was as if she'd struck him. "That's horrible."

"But you know what, there's a part of me that wonders if he was right."

"No, Claire, don't think that way." He tried to pull her into his arms again.

She stepped away, and damn it all, the tears

were back. "He insisted Colt take care of him. He didn't want me to do it because I'd done such a lousy job nursing my husband."

"He was sick in the head. He had to be."

"I know that. Just as I know I did everything in my power to help Marcus. I loved that man with every fiber of my being and I'll never love another man like that again."

That hurt him. She could see it in his eyes and she wouldn't be human if his pain didn't cause her pain, too. Still, she lifted her chin as the truth finally came out.

"I'm sorry, Ethan, but that's the truth."

"Is that so?"

She nodded.

"Then I guess there's nothing left to say."

"I guess not."

Still, he didn't leave. They stood there in silence, crickets chirping in the distance, one of the dogs crunching on food, the smell of sage filling the air. These were the things she noticed when she broke Ethan McCall's heart—because that was exactly what she'd done, and if she were honest with herself, it broke a piece of her own heart, too.

"I hope you find happiness, Claire. I hope Adam is all right."

"He will be." Because by the grace of God, she wouldn't lose another thing she loved. Not ever again.

"I'm sure you're right." He moved forward, and she could see that his hands shook and she knew she was responsible for that and it dug at her heart and made her want to vomit, but it was for the best. What she did was for both of them. He would see that in time.

"Goodbye, Claire."

He kissed her cheek. That was all he did before he turned and walked out of her life.

Chapter Nineteen

It was for the best.

The words were her mantra when the next day dawned. For the best, even though it felt like a divorce. He'd asked for Thor. She'd given him the dog without a qualm, but since he didn't plan on driving out to Montana, he'd arranged for shipping. Thus the dog would be in her care for a few more days.

It was Adam who cried when he heard Thor was leaving. Or maybe he cried over the loss of Ethan. He'd been floored by the news that his friend would be gone, and then had been so recalcitrant that it'd been hard to get to the bottom of his moodiness. She, however, had nothing to cry about. She was the one who'd ended it, and thank goodness, too. Look at how Adam had reacted. What if they'd been living together, or worse, married, and it'd all fallen apart?

And would you have married him?

It was the voice, the ever-present voice that had asked the question, the one she always ignored. She did exactly that once again.

"Do you think he thinks about us?"

There was no need to ask who Adam was talking about. They'd just been discussing Thor and the fact that he was due to be shipped out tomorrow. Mariah would be over later today to do a health certificate. Until then they were in the middle of cleaning dog kennels, the only bummer about being well again, Adam claimed: chores.

"I think he's too busy to give us much thought."

She received updates through Colt. Her

brother and Ethan had remained friends and so she knew he'd already had his stuff shipped out from his storage unit, something he'd never done while living in Via Del Caballo, which just went to show that he'd never really been serious about living on the ranch. She'd heard he loved working with the dogs. That his new boss was a dream. That he was happy to be back in the same state as his parents.

He had a sister. She hadn't even known that. Funny how you could be intimate with someone and yet not even know the basic facts about their life.

"What do I do with the food Thor didn't eat?"

She'd been so engrossed in her thoughts she hadn't even noticed that Adam had moved on to the next kennel. That he stood in the outdoor run, a shovel in his hand.

Food? "What food?"

"The food in his bowl."

She just about dropped the shovel she'd been

holding. Instead she rested it against the wall of the kennel she'd been cleaning, and then headed to Thor's enclosure.

"Doesn't look like he ate any of it," her son observed.

No. It didn't. She bent to examine the bowl. No ants. Sometimes they swarmed the food to the point that the dogs wouldn't touch it. It wasn't super warm out that day, either. Sunny, yes, but cool enough that heat shouldn't have affected his appetite. She moved to the doorway of Thor's dog run. The canine had assumed a position she recognized from before. Sad. Depressed. Not happy.

"Shit."

"Mom!"

She waved her son's complaint away. Okay. So not a big deal. Thor was upset. Ethan had left. Thor probably thought he was gone forever, like his last master. There was just one little niggling fear. He'd coughed a little yesterday.

Not a lot, and he'd quickly stopped, but it was just enough...

"What's wrong with him?" Adam asked.

"I don't know, but I'm glad Mariah is coming later today."

Unfortunately, Mariah was as puzzled as she was. "His lungs sound fine. Are you sure you heard him cough? It wasn't a gag on food or something?"

"I'm sure."

Mariah frowned, her red hair so curly she looked like something out of a Disney movie. "Well, I don't think he's got fluid in them if you were thinking canine distemper, but there's no way to know for sure unless I x-ray him. Did you feed him anything different?"

She knelt down by the dog, her mass of red hair pulled back into a ponytail, her belly big enough it was a wonder she could get up and down.

"Nope. Same food as always."

Mariah nodded, pulling out her stethoscope. "Any chance a raccoon might have gotten into it? Or maybe vermin? They can leave feces behind that can put an animal off the taste."

Claire just shot her a look before saying, "Mariah. Really. When have I ever not taken care of the food that I feed my animals?"

"Just asking," she said, moving the stethoscope. "Never hurts."

No, it didn't, but she was grasping at straws. When she finished moving the stethoscope around, Mariah stood, and Claire could tell it wasn't easy for her.

"Lord, I feel like I swallowed a swimming pool."

Claire eyed her friend. "Not to be mean, but you look like you swallowed an ocean."

"And I'm only six months pregnant," she all but wailed. "Every other woman I've ever known didn't even look pregnant at six months, but me, no, I'm as big as a whale."

"A cute whale," she placated.

"Thanks."

She waited for her friend's prognosis, but it took her a moment between bending back and placing her hands on her hips and moaning in complaint.

"Well?" she prompted.

"I have no idea."

"Really?"

Mariah had the grace to appear abashed. "Everything sounds great. Good gut noises. His lungs are clear. Heart rate normal. I see no reason why he'd be off his feed."

"They why isn't he eating?"

"He's probably missing Ethan."

"You think he's pining?"

"Maybe. It's possible he ate something bad. Or that he's choking from scarfing down too much food. Or that he's caught some kind of bug. Unfortunately, that requires blood work and that I can't do out here. I mean, I can draw it, but you might as well just bring him in. That way I can x-ray him if need be."

That was *not* the news Claire wanted to hear. Usually she could diagnose her own animals. Only in extreme circumstances did she have to bring an animal into a clinic. That it was Thor that suffered right now made it even harder to stomach. What would she tell Ethan?

"When should I bring him in?"

"Today, if possible." Mariah stretched again. "Bring him in after I finish my farm calls. Should be around four."

She hated to wait that long, but she knew Mariah was the best in the business.

A few hours later, however, X-rays didn't reveal anything. No obstructions. No swollen organs. No crazy growths.

"I don't know what to tell you," Mariah said as they stood in front of her laptop peering at the X-rays. "He must be drinking, because his electrolytes are still good. And the markers on his blood panel all look normal."

"He's pining for Ethan."

"It's totally possible, but it's also possible that he has something going on inside that we just can't see. Not yet at least. Give him a few more days."

She wasn't happy with the news. "So no health certificate, then?"

"Not yet. Not until he's eating normally. I can't risk that he might be coming down with something."

Just as she feared. That meant having to call Ethan and to explain the situation, something she didn't want to do, but that she knew was a necessity as a responsible kennel owner.

But as it turned out, she didn't have to call Ethan. Colt offered to do it, and she was just coward enough to take him up on the offer. But when her brother called her back a short while later, she wasn't so happy with his news.

"He's flying out."

"But he doesn't need to."

"I don't think he cares," said her brother. "He's doing it anyway."

HE COULDN'T GET there fast enough. When Colt had called and told him the news he hadn't hesitated. He'd hung up, called airlines and paid the astronomical price to get there the next day. Thor needed him, and his new boss understood.

Still, it felt like a week later though, in fact, it was less than twenty-four hours when he pulled to a stop next to Claire's van. She wasn't in her house. She was out in the kennel with Thor and his heart stopped when he saw the dog lying outside. Surely he'd seen him drive up. Granted, he wouldn't recognize his rental car, but when he stepped out of the vehicle, he would know.

The dog didn't move.

His heart dropped. His eyes fell upon Claire next. She tried to smile. Even from a distance he spotted the attempt, and it killed him to see her there, clearly upset, clearly wanting to ease his fears, unable to do so.

"Mariah looked at him yesterday," she said, the moment he entered the kennel, and it was all he could do not to go to her and put his arms around her. She didn't want him. Fine. He could keep his distance. "She said just to wait and see, and she's the best veterinarian I know, so I trust her."

"Yeah, but she doesn't know Thor like I do."

He had her on that point and she knew it because she didn't protest when he knelt down next to his dog. Thor hardly lifted his head.

"Hey, buddy."

Only when he touched him did he perk up. He looked into Thor's eyes and saw the recognition dawn. His black tail began to thump, but there was no effusive greeting, no open mouth smile, no pricked ears. Thor just stared and in that gaze he caught a look…

His heart stopped.

It was a nearly human plea for help. "He's sick."

"I know, but he doesn't have a fever, and his blood work came back fine. Mariah ruled out a virus and she said his white cell count looked fine so she's not thinking cancer. He's just… listless."

He instantly went to work, opening Thor's mouth. Gum color good. No extra saliva indicating his stomach might hurt. No abscessed teeth.

"Do you have a thermometer?"

"He doesn't have a fever."

"Not yet, but I'm betting he will sooner or later."

Green eyes held his gaze and he marveled at their beauty. It might have been only a few days, but it was as if he'd never seen her before. Black hair. Soft red lips. Honey and vanilla.

Claire.

"I'll go get it."

He nodded, though his hands had started to shake, but it wasn't because of anxiety. It was being around Claire, he suddenly realized. She was it. His soul mate. And he just then realized it.

"It's okay," he told Thor, although he spoke more to himself than to the dog. He would fix Thor up, and then head back to Montana because that's what she wanted.

"Here," she said, handing him a plastic tube that contained a canine thermometer. She helped to hold the dog while he checked to see if he had a fever. When he read the digital readout, he thought he'd misread it.

One hundred and four degrees.

Shit.

"What does it say?"

He showed her the thermometer. "Shit," she echoed his thoughts.

"I'm going to need access to an X-ray and an

ultrasound. Whatever's causing his infection might show up now on a scan."

"Mariah told me to bring him back today. Let's just go."

"Where's Adam?" he asked as he scooped Thor up, the big dog heavy in his arms, but he didn't care.

"At Colt's."

Good, one less thing to worry about. He glanced down at Thor. The fact that the dog didn't struggle was another indicator of just how sick he was. He didn't feel well enough to move and so he instantly relaxed in his arms.

That was the moment Ethan felt the first twinge of panic.

He'll be okay.

He tried to convince himself. Usually he was the optimist. He really had meant it when he'd told Claire to stop fearing the worst, but that was before she'd sent him away, so he was running a little low on optimism right now, and Thor only added to the mix.

They arrived at the clinic in record time, mostly because Claire drove like a crazy woman. She'd had him call to warn her friend they were on their way, so when they pulled up to the back door of a single-story wood building, it instantly opened, and a woman with a mass of red hair greeted him.

"You must be Dr. McCall."

He recognized the woman's voice from the phone. "And you must be Dr. Johnson."

"I am." She was so pregnant her lab coat didn't cover her bump. "I'd say it was a pleasure. But it's not a pleasure to meet under these circumstances." She waddled to the back of the van.

"No. It's not."

They worked in tandem, though Ethan did all the lifting. He liked that they seemed to read each other's minds when it came to diagnosing the dog. Together they went through the necessary steps to figure out what was wrong.

They came up empty.

"It's not cancer," Mariah said after looking at his blood work for the tenth time. Claire just stood back and watched and it occurred to him that she had a lot of experience with that. How many times had she done the same thing, first for her husband and then for her son?

"At least I don't see anything to indicate that," Mariah added.

He'd scanned the same test results and came up with the same answer. No cancer indicators. Not a virus. Definitely an infection of some sort, they just couldn't find it. Short of opening him up and doing exploratory surgery there was nothing they could do. They would have to wait to see if the infection that clearly wreaked havoc on his body would eventually show itself. Could be a tiny stone in his kidneys, or a foreign body, or a staph infection. Lord knew what it could be, just that Thor was sick and growing more ill by the moment.

"We can keep him in the back," Mariah told him.

They'd given Thor a sedative, not that he needed it. It just made things easier when dealing with X-rays and scans.

"I'm sorry," Claire said once they settled Thor into an oversize crate.

"What are you sorry for?" he asked, stepping back.

"This happened on my watch."

"And you noticed he was off before whatever this is manifested itself into a fever."

"Actually, it was Adam who noticed he hadn't finished his food."

"And you didn't just dismiss it as an upset stomach."

Lord, it was hard not to pull her into his arms. He wanted to console her so badly it was a physical ache. Any doubt that he wasn't in love with her had disappeared the moment he'd spotted her kneeling by his dog's side. If anything, time away had made him love her all the more. She just didn't love him, though. Would never love him. The words still stung to the point that he had to look away.

"Did you need me to stay?" she asked.

"No," he said sharply. Too sharply. He looked up, spotted the hurt in her eyes. "I'm sorry. Just worried about Thor."

"I understand."

Yes, she did. If anyone understood what it was like to fear for something you loved, she did.

"I've got it from here. You can get back to Adam."

"Actually, Colt is watching Adam and he'll be just fine there. I don't want to leave, either."

"It may be hours before we know anything. At this point it's just a waiting game."

"I'm good at waiting."

He would bet that was true, too, and it broke his heart all over again.

"I just don't understand," he heard her say. "He's been doing so well. I've been taking him for walks out behind Colt's property and he loves it. His favorite game is to play hide-and-seek in the weeds."

He could picture Thor doing that. Could imagine him crouching down behind—

He jerked upright. "Wait. You've been walking him where?"

"Out behind Colt's property. We follow the creek, and then I turn back and we walk across the big pasture."

"Son of a—"

"What?"

"There are foxtails out in that pasture. I saw them that day I walked with you."

"I know, but they're everywhere, and animals usually sneeze like crazy when that happens."

"Sometimes. Sometimes not. And it's not something we've checked for."

He saw recognition dawn. "Then we probably should."

They found Mariah in the back room washing blood off her hand.

"I hate small animals," Mariah said, showing them a dog bite. Or maybe a cat bite. "What's up? You two look anxious. Thor okay?"

"Foxtail," was all Ethan said.

She lifted a brow. "I checked him for that when he came in."

"In his throat or in his nose?"

"Just his nose." She shook her head. "To tell you the truth I ruled it out pretty quickly because he wasn't sneezing or coughing or gagging."

"Yeah, but I've seen shrapnel get stuck in some pretty crazy places. No symptoms other than they get sick as the foreign body becomes infected, kind of like what we're dealing with now." He turned to Claire. "Colt said on the phone he coughed a little the other day."

"He did." And her spirits sank. "When we were out on that walk."

He turned back to Mariah. "Do you have an esophagoscope?"

"Of course."

"Mind if I use it?"

"No. Of course not."

Mariah bandaged her finger—compliments of a cat, she explained—while her assistant, a girl named Alyssa, helped them set up. It didn't take long, but it did mean putting Thor under general anesthesia, which meant waiting for the muscle relaxant they'd given him to wear off. As the minutes ticked by and Ethan had to wait, he became more and more convinced of his diagnosis. It all fit. The brief coughing spasm. Foxtails, especially the small ones, could act like darts. They could lodge themselves into the wall of an esophagus like a thumbtack. It would hurt to swallow, which would put Thor off his food. Depending on where it was lodged, he wouldn't cough anymore, either, just be in pain. Then the infection would set in…

"It'll be okay." Claire touched his arm. "He's in good hands between you and Mariah."

It was just a dog, he reminded himself, but caring for that dog, trying to fix him up—it brought it all back. His time in the field. Watching dog after dog fight for their life. The chaos and madness and sadness of practicing medicine on animals that were soldiers, most of them wounded in the field. No wonder he didn't want to go back into practice. He didn't like the memories that came along with doing what he used to do. Much easier to focus on breeding dogs. And training dogs. That way he didn't have to remember, or be reminded.

Claire moved. He barely noticed. She tried to slip her arms beneath his own. He didn't want her to touch him. It was hell to want her and know that she didn't want him back.

She had told him she could never love another man the way she had loved Marcus. Her words still cut with the sting of a razor. But somehow she wiggled her way through, and he couldn't stop from holding her back. It felt good. So damn good. She was his anchor. The one thing on Earth that kept him sane. The cement that kept his feet on the ground. The one thing that could always soothe his anxious mind.

"We should be good to—" Mariah drew up short when she spotted Claire in his arms.

He pushed her away, and it was one of the hardest things he'd ever had to do. "Let's do it."

Chapter Twenty

He'd pushed her away.

Claire told herself that she deserved it. She was the one who'd broken things off with him. Who'd hurt him. Who continued to hurt him because it was clear he still had feelings for her. She just hoped they could still be friends.

He's way more than a friend.

She shut the door on the thought. She knew what she felt for him, and it wasn't love. It couldn't be love. She didn't have the heart to love someone again.

"Ready?" she heard Mariah ask.

Somehow they'd prepped Thor without her

noticing. The dog lay sprawled on a stainless steel table, prone, the IV still attached to his leg. She forced herself to focus. She wanted to help, although between Mariah and Ethan and no less than two veterinary technicians, she felt like a third wheel. No. A fifth wheel.

"Here we go," Ethan said, inserting the scope down Thor's throat. The video screen filled with an image that looked like the inside of a giant, pink worm. The opening was wide at first and then narrower and narrower until all that she could see was the pink and the white. He fished the probe down slowly, and Claire knew both he and Mariah were scanning the digital screen for signs of anything out of place. As it turned out, they needn't have worried because the brushy tip of a foxtail was obvious even to her.

"Look at that," Mariah said in relief.

Ethan just nodded. "The wound is infected, too. Been bleeding into his stomach."

"No wonder he isn't interested in eating,"

Mariah said. "He's had a stomach full of yuck. Not to mention, that has to hurt."

"Can you pull it out?" Claire asked.

"I'm going to try." Ethan straightened. "Unless you'd like to do it," he said to Mariah.

Mariah leaned back, patting her belly. "Are you kidding? I don't think I could get close enough to the table to do a good enough job."

That wasn't true, but it was clear Mariah had complete confidence in Ethan. And why wouldn't she? He'd been a veterinarian on the front lines. Emergency situations were nothing new to him. She could tell by the way he handled himself.

"Okay, let's do it, then."

"You'll need to get hold of it by the bottom," Mariah said, a frown on her face as she watched. "Those things are notorious for coming out in pieces."

"I know."

He moved the probe this way and that by

twisting it around. He got the thing a little closer to the base of the foxtail, the resolution on the screen refreshing and instantly changing so that the image was sharper.

"That's amazing." She'd never watched a vet use a probe before and she was fascinated by Ethan's expertise. In a matter of minutes he had the thing where he wanted, squeezed on something on his end, the tiny ends closing, Ethan pulling back…

Out it popped.

There were audible sighs all around. Claire resisted the urge to shout. If Ethan hadn't been able to remove the thing it would have meant surgery and that added a layer of risk that a sick dog didn't need.

"Thank goodness," Mariah said with a wide smile.

He placed the seed pod in his hand. Such an innocuous weed, yet so deadly.

"I'm sorry," she said again.

"What are you sorry for?" Mariah asked.

"I was the one taking him on walks." To think about Ethan. To try to understand why she felt so empty inside. "I heard him cough. I should have kept a closer eye on him."

Mariah moved to her side. "You had no way of knowing what happened. Most dogs inhale these things through their nose. It's crazy that it went down his throat, but it's good. Much easier to fix." She patted her on the back. "You are not to blame."

"We'll need to monitor him," Ethan said. "I don't like how infected the area looked."

"We can keep him overnight," Mariah said.

"I would appreciate that."

"I'll call Colt and ask if you can stay there again," Claire offered.

"No. That's okay. I can stay in a hotel."

She had no reason to feel hurt, no reason at all, but she did. "You don't have to do that."

No. But he would, because breaking up with

her had hurt and she could see the lingering evidence of that hurt in his eyes.

"Well, okay," Mariah said, clearly sensing the tension in the air. "I'll have my receptionist make some calls for you, then. There's a few hotels nearby."

He held her gaze for a split second longer, and in his eyes she spotted anger and sadness and a plea for something. Then he tore his gaze away and looked at Mariah. "I'd appreciate that."

She found herself backing away from him.

"Do you mind bringing Thor out of anesthesia?" Mariah asked. "I have a patient to see in the front."

"I don't mind at all."

"I think I'm going to leave."

They both turned to look at her, Mariah's expression turning to one of concern. "Are you okay?"

"Fine," she said with a mouth so dry it was like swallowing the Southern California desert.

"You look a little sick," Mariah observed.

"I'm fine," she repeated. "Just going to head on out of here so I'm not in the way."

And so I can't see the sadness in Ethan's eyes. Sadness and regret. Love and understanding. Desire and regret. And she felt it, too.

She turned away from her friend so quickly she almost slipped on the tile floor. She ran toward the back door without another word. When she burst outside, she sucked in a breath because she couldn't breathe all of a sudden.

You're losing it, said that little voice.

No. She wasn't losing it. She was just admitting the truth. It wasn't that she *didn't* love Ethan. It was that she did. Dear Lord. She loved him. And he was so disappointed in her. She could see it in his eyes. And he didn't want anything more to do with her and it was all her fault. She'd pushed him away.

Because you're a coward.

She tipped forward, resting her hands on her

knees. No. She was afraid. A coward would jump in a car and drive away and never look back, never admit how much the thought of loving him scared her because it meant opening herself up to the risk of loss. Again. She didn't think she'd survive another heartbreak.

You can't think like that.

It was Ethan's voice that she heard in her head, his words so soft and gentle that she squeezed her eyes shut.

"Claire?"

She stood quickly, the change in altitude causing her vision to blur and for her to sway. He stepped forward and caught her before she fell.

"Claire, what's the matter? Was it the procedure? You looked ready to pass out in there."

She stood there for a moment, her throat swollen, unsure what to say, a part of her wanting to push him away, another part of her wanting to collapse in his arms.

"Claire?" he said, and she saw it then. He didn't hate her. He still loved her. A lot.

She had to take a deep breath, had to steel her heart as she looked into his eyes.

"I love you," she whispered.

She felt him stiffen, but she rushed on. "I love you and I told you to go away and I'm such an idiot, because it took me until right now, right this very second, to recognize the truth."

His eyes were steady as they searched hers, but he didn't say anything, just held her gently.

"And I'm scared."

Only then did he move, and it was so he could rest a palm against the side of her face, the gesture so familiar from their night of lovemaking and so dear that she felt tears come to her eyes.

"You don't have to be scared," he said softly.

"But what if I lose you?"

There it was. Her worst fear. The one that kept her from telling him to stay and from falling into his arms.

His other hand lifted. "You might." He cupped her face. "And I might lose you, too."

She shook her head.

"No. Don't shake your head. I might lose you, Claire. Neither one of us knows how much time we have."

"Ethan."

"And so, in a way, I'm just as scared as you are."

She blinked. "You are?"

He nodded, green eyes filled with tenderness and something else. "Terrified. But I'm tired of being afraid, Claire. When I came back from the Middle East my hands shook for weeks. I couldn't sleep at night. I had nightmares." He looked down. "I still have nightmares," he confessed, but then his gaze connected with hers again. "But you helped me to see that no matter what happens, no matter how much we lose, it's worth it to fight."

She forced herself to breathe. "I did?"

He leaned his head down close to hers. "You're the bravest woman I know, Claire."

"No, I'm not."

"Then let me be there for you," he said. "Let me carry the weight of your worries."

His words took her breath away.

"I love you," he said, rocking her, holding her, trying to reassure her. "Leaving you was the hardest thing I've ever had to do in my life. It was like dying myself. Don't make me live without you, Claire, because that's something to fear. That's a life I don't want to lead."

"Oh, Ethan."

He leaned back again. "I love you, Claire Reynolds. I have no idea what tomorrow will bring—nobody does—but I know I don't want to face it without you by my side."

She started to cry. He wiped the tears away.

"I don't want to, either," she confessed.

He started to smile. "Good."

She started to smile, too, because she was

tired of fighting her feelings for him. She'd been fighting them since the first moment she'd seen him standing there on the tarmac, sadness stamped into his face. Fighting them when she'd watched him work with the dogs, so kind to them and gentle. Fighting them when he took care of her. Fighting them as she watched him work with her son.

"I love you," he said again.

"I love you, too," she said.

"Marry me?" he asked.

She closed her eyes, warm tears falling. She gave up then. She would give him her fears, just as he asked, and her heart. She reached up on tiptoe and kissed him, and it was funny, because it was as if his love poured into her soul. That love washed the fear and sorrow and sadness of the past away. A moment later, when she looked into his eyes, even more tears fell. It was *her* turn for happiness. *Her* turn for a marriage that lasted a lifetime—that was the promise in his eyes.

And for once, she believed.

Epilogue

"Mom! Mom! Mom! Wake up! It's happening."

Claire sat up so fast, she clocked her elbow against the lamp sitting on her nightstand. "Ouch," she cried, blindly grasping for the thing before it crashed to the floor.

"Hurry," Adam added, the crack of light that stretched from the bedroom door seeming to slice the room in half.

"I'm coming, I'm coming," she murmured sleepily, glancing at the clock. Two o'clock in the morning. Of course it would have to be at 2 a.m. Wasn't that when every pregnant mother gave birth? She glanced at the spot where Ethan had lain next to her earlier that evening. He'd been called out to a farm and actually he was the one that insisted babies—even the furry kind—always seemed to know when nobody was around.

"Who called?" she yelled to her son, but he was already gone, probably off to get dressed. How had she not heard the house phone?

You're exhausted.

Planning a wedding. Organizing a baby shower. Traveling between her place and Ethan's. They didn't want to live together. Not until they were married. It'd surprised her how old-fashioned Ethan turned out to be when it came right down to it. He even refused to live at Colt and Natalie's place, insisting he get a place of his own. So they sneaked around behind Adam's back, keeping their visits short, although tonight's visit had been preempted with Ethan leaving before Adam came home from spending time with his aunt and uncle. It was hell, but she'd set a date around Christmastime. Chance would be out of the Army by then. She'd have her whole family around her, including Natalie and Colt's new baby.

Speaking of that...

She hurriedly pulled on her clothes. No time to doll herself up, at least not according to Adam, who practically bounced on his toes.

"Took you long enough."

She ignored him, even though inside she smiled at his impatience. There was little doubt her son was on the mend. His blood tests continued to show no signs of cancer, so much so that they were told not to come back to the doctor for another six months. By the time she and Ethan were married she hoped to receive the gift of her son's official remission. Adam's doctor seemed to think that was more than probable. And one thing she'd learned during this whole ordeal—doctors didn't say things like that unless they were pretty darn sure.

"Have you heard from Ethan?" She started her van, glancing over at the row of kennels. Thor's was empty. The former combat dog had become Ethan's constant companion. Ethan took him everywhere, even when he was called out at night.

"That's who called."

So he was already at the hospital. Good.

They arrived in record time, although not fast enough for Adam, who raced through the clinic's back door. She raced, too, if she were honest with herself, because now that the time was finally here she couldn't wait to see what the stork would bring them.

"Is she okay?" Adam asked when he spotted Ethan standing by a room off to the side of the main examination area.

"It's all looking good." He caught her eyes and his smile did the same thing to her that it always did. It made her insides warm and her spirits lift in a way that always seemed to make her feel less troubled, less anxious—and loved. "I think she's going to be okay."

Claire moved up next to him, peering into the room that was lined with kennels, one at the end containing a female Belgian Malinois that panted as if she'd run a mile.

Thor's babies were about to be born.

As if sensing his impending fatherhood, Thor stood in the middle of the room, a low-pitched whine barely audible above the drone of the electronic equipment in the exam room.

"So no C-section?"

Ethan wrapped an arm around her, drawing her close, a smile on his face as he stared down at her. "I don't think so. I did an ultrasound when I noticed she was dilated and I actually think she's going to be okay. All that worry for nothing, although I'm glad we kept her here just in case."

They'd been worried that as a maiden bitch she might have trouble delivering. It was common to Belgian Malinois, being more slight of frame than their German shepherd cousins.

"Well, I'm glad you looked in on her before going home."

He nodded. "Going to be a long night."

"But you're used to it."

He was the hardest-working man she'd ever met. Once he'd made the choice to go back into veterinary work he'd thrown himself into it whole hog. Mariah couldn't stop singing his praises. Together they'd increased their client base by 50 percent—in just a few months. They were already talking about bringing on another veterinarian. Ethan even had someone in mind, a friend of his from the Army.

"I'm used to it, but it'll make for a long day tomorrow."

She nodded in sympathy, only to jump when the back door burst open, a pregnant Natalie sailing through the door. Her sister-in-law was one of those women who didn't look pregnant, not yet at least, unlike Mariah, who'd given birth to a healthy baby boy a few weeks ago. It was why Mariah had brought Ethan on board, although she'd long since asked to make it permanent. Ethan had accepted and so the Via Del Caballo Veterinary Hospital had a new partner.

"Well?"

"I can't believe you came down here," Claire said.

"Are you kidding? I wasn't going to miss this. That's my bitch in there."

The words sounded so funny they all laughed. Natalie had purchased the female Belgian based on Ethan's recommendation. She wanted a dog to help protect the ranch and the precious number of high-dollar horses they cared for, but she didn't want to take a dog from Claire's program, and since Ethan wanted a breed, a plan had been born. Four months later that plan was about to happen.

"Well?" Colt asked, bursting in next.

"Nothing yet," Ethan said.

Her brother wore his usual denim shirt and black cowboy hat. He caught her gaze and shot his gaze heavenward before saying, "You'd have thought we were on the way to the birth of Jesus."

"I can't wait to see what my baby's babies look like," Natalie said.

"You say that now, but wait until you have to take care of them all," Colt said.

"How could you not love taking care of puppies? Besides, they'll be at Claire's until they're big enough to come home."

She clearly had him there, and Claire had to smile. If she and Ethan shared half the love her brother shared with his wife, they'd be the luckiest people on Earth.

As if sensing her thoughts, Ethan's gaze caught her own, his eyes softening, and there it was again, the feeling of peace and happiness and contentment.

"Something's happening," Adam said.

They'd talked about banning him from the birthing room, but it wasn't as if her son hadn't seen cows born in the pasture, and so her six-year-old stared transfixed as Lady went to work. Ethan moved in close. Natalie moved to the head of her dog, soothing her. She'd owned the dog for four months, but it was clear they were already bonded.

"It's a boy!" Ethan announced.

"Whoo-hoo," Adam said. "My own Thor."

As if he could hear his name, the father of the puppies whined again. Claire smiled and patted his head. Soon Natalie would be giving birth. Then it would be their turn. With any luck, she and Ethan would have a child of their own next year.

As if sensing the direction of her thoughts, Ethan met her gaze again, a puppy cuddled in his arms. She didn't know why, but the sight of her big handsome military hero holding that tiny bundle of fur made her heart flip over backward. He smiled. She did, too, her eyes misting up as she watched her family huddle around the dog, even Colt assisting at one point. Nine puppies later, Lady was all done, mom and puppies resting quietly while brother, sister, wife, fiancé and son looked on.

"That'll be you soon," Colt said to Natalie.

"Good Lord, I hope not. If I give birth to nine babies someone will need to shoot me."

They all chuckled. Claire felt a hand on her back. She looked into Ethan's eyes. She knew he was thinking the same thing she was. One day they would be pregnant. One day Adam would have a brother or a sister. One day their family would be complete. It might not happen next year. It might not happen for a while, but Claire was okay with that. They had their whole life ahead of them.

"I love you," he silently mouthed.

She smiled, lifted her head, kissed him as a way of answering back.

Adam snuggled up next to them. Her hand fell on his shoulder and in that moment, that exact second, Claire knew the dark days were behind her. It was as if God gave her a glimpse into the future, a moment of clarity in which she somehow knew that it would all work out. Adam would be cured. Ethan would love her forever. And if there were bumps in the road, their love would carry them through.

And it always did.

* * * * *

MILLS & BOON®

Why shop at millsandboon.co.uk?

Each year, thousands of romance readers find their perfect read at millsandboon.co.uk. That's because we're passionate about bringing you the very best romantic fiction. Here are some of the advantages of shopping at www.millsandboon.co.uk:

* **Get new books first**—you'll be able to buy your favourite books one month before they hit the shops

* **Get exclusive discounts**—you'll also be able to buy our specially created monthly collections, with up to 50% off the RRP

* **Find your favourite authors**—latest news, interviews and new releases for all your favourite authors and series on our website, plus ideas for what to try next

* **Join in**—once you've bought your favourite books, don't forget to register with us to rate, review and join in the discussions

Visit **www.millsandboon.co.uk**
for all this and more today!